The Treasure of the Turkish Pasha

The Treasure of the Turkish Pasha

by Yehoash Biber   Pictures by Uri Shulevitz

Translated from the Hebrew by Baruch Hochman

Charles Scribner's Sons   *New York*

Contents

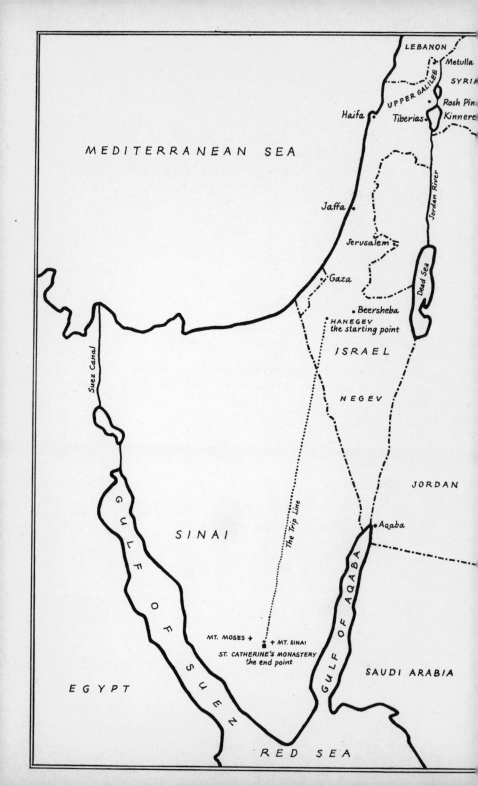

Part I

Plans

1

Night Visitors

It was late when I heard a soft knock at the door of my house. I had come in after settling Beauty in the stable and had locked the door for the night. I was working as a guard at Hanegev, a village on the northern border of the Negev. My companions on watch in those days were Beauty, my mare, and my police dog, Dana.

I had slipped the rifle off my shoulder and was hanging it in its place on the wall when I heard the knock, then another, and another. I stood still, all ears. Fierce Bedouin tribes surrounded the settlement, and the outlaws among them, some of whom had felt the strength of my right arm, had become my sworn enemies. Were night visitors waiting for me to open up so they could pick me off as I stood in the doorway? Who could it be so late at night?

Dana growled softly.

I drew my pistol, loaded, and cocked it. Then I moved to the side of the door.

"Who's there?" I asked.

"Open, and we'll tell you."

"O.K. The door is unlatched."

I stood back, pistol in hand. If the strangers outside tried to shoot, they wouldn't hit me, since I stood behind the door. If they began to shoot after they entered the room, I was in a position to pick them off.

The hinges creaked and groaned; the door moved slowly and opened. Two men entered. One was tall, with a great mane of silver hair and a broad, flat briefcase in his hand. The other was short, stocky and broad shouldered. He was wearing an old black leather jacket.

The two men looked around.

"Anyone here?" the tall one called.

"Who are you?" I asked from behind the door.

They turned back to find themselves looking into the barrel of my pistol.

"Oh!" the tall one cried.

"Don't shoot. We're friends," the other said.

"So late at night? At such an hour, only people in bad trouble come to see me—or enemies."

The short man laughed. "You'll soon find out," he said in a deep voice, "that there's still a third kind of night visitor. May we sit down?" he asked and pointed to the chairs by the table.

"If you are friends, as you say, welcome. Sit down."

I put the pistol back in its holster. The two men seated themselves at the table. The tall one held on to his portfolio.

"Will you have some coffee?" I asked. I'm an old hand

at brewing Bedouin coffee. I learned how to make it in the tents of Kedar, during my long years as a guardsman.

"Yes," the tall one said. "We'd like to have some."

I shut the door and drew the bolt. I knew Dana would warn me if a stranger approached, but it always pays to be careful.

Dana rolled onto the heap of soft, old rags that served as her bed. She was a splendid beast—and a superb watchdog. I had trained her myself. She would eat only from my hand and only on my orders. Even if offered the most tempting morsel, she wouldn't touch it without a signal from me.

Once, when I was away tracking down marauders, I was forced to leave Dana alone for three whole days. There was enough food in her dish, but she didn't touch it. She was starved when I returned but wouldn't eat until I told her to. Then she wolfed it all down in record time. There was one other person she would take orders from, and that was my son Gil. At the time of the treasure hunt he was just fifteen.

I lit my little kerosene stove and put a kettle of water on to boil. My guests sat silently at the table.

While the water is boiling, I will tell you who I am.

For years now I've been a member of the *Shomrim*, the Guards. I was a Guardsman back in the days when the Turks ruled the country. Ever since our organization was founded, it has been our job to protect outlying Jewish settlements. Everywhere in Palestine, and beyond its borders, they call me Abu-Gil-Shatter—that is, Father-of-Gil, the Brave. I'm not boasting. I didn't choose the name. My real name is Jeremiah Hanegbi, and my friends call me Yirmi, or "the Negev man." I've always loved the Negev, with its wide-open spaces, its Bedouin tribes, and the wild animals that wander freely over its wastes.

I have many friends in the Negev, some of them famous sheikhs who rule over great tribes of Bedouin. They are brave hunters, nomads who often smuggle contraband goods in and out of the country. Friendship with outlaws can be very useful to a man like me; it's better to be their friend than their enemy.

My comrades in the Guards considered me their "Negev man." They were always sending me on missions in this area. I have traveled far and wide in all the deserts of the Middle East, and I know them well—their trails, their oases, their various tribes, and their animals.

As a young man, when I was still guarding the fields of a village in Upper Galilee, I married Hannah. She died giving birth to Gil, my only son. She was a good woman, and a loyal one. I too am loyal, to her and to her memory; I have not married again.

I brought Gil up by myself. From his earliest days, I taught him to handle rifle, pistol, and dagger; he became accustomed to long, difficult journeys on horseback, by donkey and camel back. Like me, he can follow a desert track. He speaks Arabic like a native, and he is well-versed in the ways of our neighbors, in their customs, and in the traditions of their fathers. He has often joined me in my adventures as a Guard.

Recently I took on this job of guarding the new settlement of Hanegev. Its members have settled here to study the climate, the soil, and the agriculture of the area, and to know the people. Others will follow them and build villages in this desolate region.

Gil, who is at an agricultural boarding school in the North, comes home only for holidays and vacations. Then he spends his time on his horse Lightning, a swift, black stallion, the gift of Suleiman Muhamad abu-Salma, the Great Sheikh of the Tarbin tribe.

The water boiled in the kettle. I added finely ground coffee and sugar and then pounded a few grains of fragrant *hel* and dropped them into the steaming pot. The Bedouin use *hel* to add flavor and aroma. I poured the coffee into three small porcelain cups and put them on a copper tray.

I brought the tray to the table and set it down. Before I pulled up a chair for myself, I gave Dana some fresh food.

"You still don't know why we've come," the tall man said, his hand on his briefcase.

"No, no! I won't talk business until you've had something to drink and rested awhile."

"Of course. Of course," the tall man said, and I noticed that he had blue eyes and a pleasant smile.

"I think we ought to introduce ourselves," he added. "For reasons you will understand later, we'll use only our first names. My name is Reuben, Ruby for short," and he shook my hand.

"My name is Yohai," the other said and also took my hand in his. His arms were heavy and muscular, and he obviously wasn't much of a talker. He had dark eyes and shaggy, black eyebrows.

We sipped our coffee in silence.

"Marvelous drink," Ruby said. "It warms you through and through."

13

After we had drunk the coffee, I invited my guests to make themselves comfortable on sofas and pillows in the *madafa*—the guest room, where I entertained distinguished visitors. I trimmed the wick in the kersone lamp, lit it, sank into an armchair, and puffed at my pipe. I inhaled the aromatic tobacco and offered cigarettes to my guests. The smoke rose and curled over our heads.

"Now, why have you come?" I asked Ruby.

"It's a long story," the tall man said, "and it has to do with a treasure."

2

Kemal Pasha's Treasure

"Before the First World War," Ruby began, "when the Turks still ruled Palestine, there was a pasha in Jerusalem called Kemal Ata-Pasha. The Turkish pashas were notorious for their cruelty. *Falakas*—whipping the soles of the feet—was a punishment meted out at every turn. Officials thought of their subjects as their private property, to do with as they wished. They confiscated their goods, condemned them to forced labor, threw them into prison, impressed them into the army, and taxed them mercilessly.

"The Turkish empire was very corrupt. Offices were sold to the highest bidder. In order to make up for the huge sums they had paid into the Sultan's treasury, officials fleeced their subjects—and practically skinned them alive in the process.

"Even among the Turks, Kemal Pasha was notorious for his brutality," Ruby said, pausing for a moment. Then he continued. "Here, in this briefcase, I have documents concerning the government of Kemal Ata-Pasha."

He opened the briefcase and took out a bundle of papers. The top sheet was marked "1" in red pencil. "These are letters he himself wrote, as well as reports on him by his superiors. I tell you, Yirmi, it was one hell of a job to find them in the Turkish archives."

"How did you know my nickname?" I interrupted. "Only my closest friends call me that."

"And the Arabs call you Abu-Gil-Shatter, right?" Then he continued his story without answering my question.

"I also found letters from Jews who lived in Jerusalem in the Pasha's days. Their contents are enough to make your hair stand on end.

"The Jews and their property were at the mercy of both the Pasha's henchmen and their Moslem neighbors. Even the Arab water carriers took advantage of them. When the carriers couldn't sell their water in the town, they would leave it with a Jew and demand payment. If he didn't pay, they would beat him up and take him to court. And whenever there was a lawsuit between a Jew and a Moslem, the judges favored the Moslem. Jews paid two and three times as many taxes as non-Jews, and new fines were constantly being imposed on them to fill Kemal Pasha's coffers.

"Many of the Jews in Palestine at the time had come from Eastern Europe. They were mostly shopkeepers and peddlers, but because it was hard for them to earn a living, they were aided by organizations called *kollelim*. Each *kollel* would collect money from charitable Jews in Europe for distribution to its members in Palestine. There were rich *kollelim* and poor ones. The members of the rich *kollelim* were pretty well off, but those of the poor ones could hardly scrape by.

"You see, Yirmi, I know a lot about those days. In civilian life, I was a history teacher."

"But you're a soldier now?" I asked.

"Not exactly," he answered. "But we'll come to that."

"Kemal Pasha," Ruby continued, "was a giant man, with a red face and an enormous moustache. He carried a whip which had three separate leather tongues, each one weighted at the tip with a piece of lead. He used the whip brutally on the slightest provocation. His greed for gold knew no limits. He had a room full of iron chests, in which he locked the gold he extorted from his subjects.

"Jerusalem had a very mixed population in those days. There were Englishmen, Frenchmen, Russians, Germans, and Austrians, besides the Arabs and the Turks, as well as Jews from a great variety of places. Therefore all kinds of monies were in circulation, and there were money changers who dealt in them. One day a group of Jewish merchants got together and organized a company which operated rather like the banks we have today. They traded in gold and had connections with banks and money changers everywhere.

"Kemal Pasha knew all about this company, of course, and harassed it for tolls and bribes.

"This is how the company operated: Shipments of coins from abroad would reach Jaffa by ship and then be transported to Jerusalem on mules. There was as yet no paved road to Jerusalem, so one had to depend on donkeys, camels, mules, and horses for transportation. The animals were guarded by armed soldiers, hired especially for the purpose, and valued highly for their loyalty to their employers.

"One day a big shipment of gold coins arrived in Jaffa.

The company's representative notified Yehoshua Halevi—he was the director of the company in Jerusalem and one of its chief stockholders—that the coins had arrived and asked that a mule team be sent to transport it."

Ruby paused to remove from his briefcase a sheet of paper marked with a red "2." "My second major document —a letter from Avraham Hai, a Sephardic Jew, who was the company's representative in Jaffa. He records the value of the shipment and includes an order bearing Yehoshua Halevi's private seal. No shipment was turned over to Halevi's agents unless they presented such a sealed order.

"Yehoshua Halevi sent his agent armed with such an order, several guards, and a team of mules to pick up the shipment, and Avraham Hai turned over to them three chests of gold. They were loaded on the donkeys, and the party started for home."

Ruby now removed document number "3" from his briefcase. It turned out to be the record of the return journey.

"The first night Halevi's men lodged at an inn in the Arab town of Lod, and next morning continued on their way. They reached the village of Artuf and then passed Bab-al-Wad, on the road to Jerusalem. Halfway between Bab-al-Wad and Jerusalem they were ambushed by a group of armed bandits on horseback. The bandits shot the guards and Yehoshua Halevi's agent; however, one guard remained alive, and although he was badly wounded he managed to escape and headed for Lod. The survivor was so stunned and confused he was unable to give a very clear picture of what had happened. But his fragmentary account, recorded by a Turkish police officer, helps us, more or less, to reconstruct the incident. Policemen from Lod hurried to the scene where the ambush had taken place but found only the bodies of the guards and the agent. The mules had disappeared, and the gold with them. According to the survivor, one of the robbers had been exceptionally tall and broad-shouldered, and the bandana on his face had not wholly concealed a bushy moustache. Though quite sure that the tall man had been the Turkish Pasha himself, the witness—probably out of fear—would not swear to it.

"Imagine what this meant to Yehoshua Halevi and his firm. Many families who depended on the money from abroad—it was called *haluka,* charity money—were threatened with starvation, since the gold was to have been distributed among the *kollelim* in the town. Yehoshua Halevi's company went bankrupt, and Yehoshua Halevi himself finally died penniless. He had borrowed money to make good the theft and spent the rest of his life paying it off.

"Now we come to the most interesting part of the story. Soon after the robbery, the Turkish Pasha disappeared—no one knows where. One of his servants reported that his master had vanished and taken with him the treasure chests he had kept hidden in his room—the chests containing gold and silver that he had extorted from his subjects during the long years of his rule. An official inquiry revealed that he had not gone back to his family in Constantinople, and that even the Turkish War office had no clue as to his whereabouts. He is on its records as a missing person to this very day."

"Why are you telling *me* all this now?"

"I'll explain that in a minute," Ruby answered. "First

let me ask you a question? What do you know about the Haganah?"

"It's an underground defense organization that protects the Jewish community against attack by its enemies."

"Everyone knows that, but you know more than that," Yohai said pointedly.

"What does that mean?" I said, becoming irritated. "Because we know that you've been a member of the Haganah for a long time. That's so, isn't it, Yirmi?"

"That's a question no one asks."

"Of course not. But don't worry about us. We're not spies."

"Nevertheless, ask me no questions, I'll tell you no lies," I replied.

"We didn't expect you to admit it, but we know you belong."

"Who told you?"

"It's very simple. We're members of the Haganah too. We belong to Haganah Intelligence. One day our chief— I won't mention his name now, for obvious reasons—called me in and showed me the most important document in this file. We call it the T.P.T. file—the Turkish Pasha's Treasure file. But first I should explain that within the Haganah Intelligence Section, there is a sub-section that deals with the restoration of stolen Jewish property to its owner. Yohai here is the head of this sub-section."

"You mean you're trying to right old wrongs," I said.

"Not exactly. Of course we like to restore stolen goods to their rightful owners. But before we take on a case, we always make an agreement with the descendants of the rightful owners to give us part of the money for a special fund."

"What kind of a fund?"

"The fund is to help bring Jews who want to come here into Palestine. It's an expensive operation and a dangerous one, since, as you know, it involves illegal immigration. The number of Jews allowed to come into the country legally by the British is hopelessly small. We also need money to buy arms for Haganah and finance our other underground activities. This is one way of getting the money. Do you agree that it's only fair that we ask for a share of the money we recover to use for such purposes?"

"Certainly," I said.

"You've probably guessed by now why we are so anxious to find the Turkish Pasha's treasure. In addition we've discovered that Yehoshua Halevi has no heirs, so everything we find can go into the fund. And we need the money desperately for urgent projects.

"I was drafted for this job because of my background in history and special interest in the period when the Turks ruled Palestine. The Chief sent for me and introduced me to Yohai, who he said would be in charge of the operations.

"I went to work on the problem. I dug up every surviving scrap of paper from that period—and learned everything I could about the life of Kemal Pasha. I found the wounded guard's testimony, indicating that Kemal Pasha had probably participated in the ambush himself.

"The T.P.T. file was full of documents, but they were far from solving the mystery of what had happened to the Turkish Pasha. Bank records of the time gave no evidence that Kemal Pasha had deposited any sum of money anywhere. And even if he hadn't organized the ambush and stolen the gold, where had his own treasure disappeared to? It is inconceivable that he could have spent so much money without leaving any trace. We've even interviewed members of the Pasha's family in Constantinople, but they, too, have no idea what had become of him.

"We came to the conclusion that there must be a connection between the theft of Halevi's gold and the Pasha's disappearance. 'It's possible,' we thought, 'that Kemal Pasha stole Yehoshua Halevi's gold, stored it with his private hoard, and intended to hide it all somewhere—or perhaps tried to smuggle it to a neighboring country.' That wouldn't have been hard to do. There are smugglers who are willing to take on such jobs for a price. But we think that at some point, while trying to get it to its hiding place or smuggle it abroad, Kemal Pasha was murdered—or died, or was kidnapped—or God knows what. The gold disappeared, and Kemal Pasha disappeared, as though the earth had swallowed them up."

"It's quite a story," I said, puffing to relight my pipe, which had gone out in the meantime. "But is this all you know about the stolen treasure?"

"No," said Ruby. "There is more."

3

The Little Black Notebook

"One day I was sitting in the National Library in Jerusalem, going through manuscripts dealing with the Turkish Pasha's regime. I'd gone through most of them dozens of times. That day I was examining a shabby old folder, and a little black notebook fell out of it. It was faded and crumpled, and its binding was mildewed. I picked it up, and a dank smell rose from its pages.

"The pages were yellow with age and covered with strange symbols in black ink. Some were so badly mildewed that I could hardly distinguish one letter from the next. The writing was obviously in code, and the code was complicated. But with the help of the Haganah's crack cryptographers we decoded it and deciphered the contents of the book.

"This is what we learned. The notebook belonged to a Jewish secret society that had been active under the Turks. Its members had decided that it was time to stand up to their persecutors. They called themselves the 'Sikorites,' after the Sikorite zealots who had fought the Romans in Jerusalem at the time of the Second Temple. The notebook contained a record of the modern Sikorites' activities. In it I found an entry dated around the time of the robbery. The entry indicated that the chests of gold were concealed near St. Catherine's Monastery in the Sinai desert. It was followed by an illegible passage, and then the statement that a map of the area, showing where the chests are to be found, is hidden in the monastery library, in the Great Prayer Book compiled in the 12th century by a Greek monk called Father Sebastian. The rest was indecipherable.

"I decided I had finally unearthed a clue worth following. I reasoned that the prayer book and the map were probably still in the library at St. Catherine's. But how and when had the map been brought to the monastery? Why had it been hidden in the prayer book? The little black notebook said nothing about that, and I suspected we'd never know, unless we got to the monastery. How the Sikorites had discovered where the treasure was hidden was another question to which I was anxious to find the answer.

"I've been involved in all sorts of mysteries, but this one stumps me. However, we figure the gold is very valuable, and we need every penny we can find."

"I can imagine," I said. "But why are you telling *me* all this? How do I fit into the picture?"

The men looked at me silently. I was busy cleaning my pipe. I poked around inside the bowl, scraping out the crusted ashes with a little metal pick. Then I took some tobacco, tamped it firmly down, and lit the pipe.

"We have a job for you to do," Ruby said finally.

"For me? I've had enough 'jobs' in my time. I'd like to

take it easy for a while. I need a little peace and quiet."

"You're the only man who can help us," Ruby said. "No one can match your knowledge of the Bedouin. You know their ways, and you have many friends among their sheikhs. You're a crack shot and a first-rate horseman— and you speak Arabic, Turkish, and English. It will take all that to get through to St. Catherine's Monastery, get hold of the map, and try to find the treasure.

"We must find the gold. We've invested a lot of time and money in this project."

The men sat silent and waited. I went out to the kitchen to boil water for more coffee while I thought it over. It was very late. I had wandered up and down the country-side for years. I'd stood guard in dozens of settlements, I'd got involved in all sorts of hassles, and helped track down bandits and assorted other criminals. I had even been away from home when Gil was born. I was tracking down a band of smugglers who had slipped across the Jordan, and I could not even be with my wife during the agoniz-ing childbirth that had cost her her life.

And now I had decided to settle down, build a house, and start a farm that Gil could think of as home. But a man can't escape his destiny. Anyone fated to be a wan-derer will never settle down. As the Arabs say, a dweller in tents is always at the mercy of the winds. I was being forced into another adventure: to penetrate the Sinai desert on treacherous trails, to find a treasure that might not even exist—that might be nothing more than a figment of someone's imagination.

The water boiled, and I served my guests fresh coffee. They sat sipping it in silence, and I sat opposite them. I went on thinking for a while, and then I said:

"Let's do it this way. You go to sleep; it's almost

25

dawn, anyway. I'll think it over and let you know in the morning."

They agreed. I made their beds, and they went to sleep. I lit my pipe again, called Dana, who sprang friskily toward me, and went to make my last rounds before morning.

The pre-dawn air was cold and fresh. My pipe glowed duskily. First I went to the barn to see my mare, Beauty, and Lightning, Gil's horse. Beauty was a thoroughbred, a *Muheladiya,* descended from the breed of Khalif Halid ben Walid, whose mares were famous throughout the East. She was a tall, sleek, powerful beast. She had small sensitive ears, a long silky mane, delicate legs, a broad chest, and a fine, slender tail.

Beauty caught my scent and whinnied happily. She rested her head on my shoulder and playfully rubbed her jaw against my shirt. She was a real friend, and a faithful one. The Arabs say there is no life without a camel, but no honor without a mare. And indeed, a mare like Beauty brought honor to her master; she was the talk of the Bedouin in the region. The Bedouin believe in a mare's luck, which they term *siasat-al-faras.* Beauty had saved my life more than once, and the Bedouin attributed it to her luck.

An Arab treasures a good horse and will look after one as carefully as he looks after his wife or daughter—sometimes more carefully. If his mare dies, he says, "I mourn you as I would a beloved daughter."

Beauty was like a daughter to me. I loved her very much.

I filled a bucket with oats and poured them into the manger. Beauty whinnied contentedly and chewed loudly. She pawed the floor as she ate. I stood and watched her for a while, and then I looked after Lightning.

He, too, was a great horse. Gil had had him since the colt was not quite a year old, and they had grown up together, the horse and the boy. Lightning had become a sturdy young stallion, with a small head, a strong supple body, and two white hind legs, like white stockings. No one but Gil and me was permitted to ride him.

I patted Lightning under the jaw, and his lips trembled with pleasure. Then I poured him some oats. The horses chewed away, and I left the barn to continue my rounds. My hand was on my holster, ready for anything. Caution was second nature to me.

The morning breezes, cool and clean, fanned my cheek and cleared my head. I turned the matter over in my mind. Finally, I decided I would take on the mission. If there was a treasure, it was important to find it. I felt better after I had made up my mind.

I whistled for Dana, who was sniffing around in the bushes, and headed homeward to sleep a little before morning.

I awoke rather late. My guests were already up and were sitting at the table. Dana got up, stretched, yawned, and went to her dish to see if there was anything left for her to eat.

We ate breakfast, Ruby, Yohai and I, without exchanging a word. But both of them watched me expectantly. I didn't open my mouth until we had finished eating. My years among the Bedouin had taught me the wisdom of the desert: that haste is unseemly, and that you don't do business until your guests have eaten and relaxed.

When breakfast was over, I invited them to sit in the shade of the mulberry tree in the yard. Then I gave them my answer.

"I've thought it over, and I've decided to do it."

"That's marvelous, Yirmi," Ruby cried. "If you take it on, I'm sure you'll succeed."

"*Inshailah,* as the Arab says," I replied. "God willing, we'll manage it—somehow."

"Excellent," said Yohai.

"But I make one condition: I must choose my own party and decide how to set about finding the treasure."

"Fine," said Ruby. "We'll provide everything you need."

"I'll make a list. While you're assembling what we need, I'll do a little traveling and round up my men."

It took me all morning to draw up the list. I had to include everything we would possibly need. Once underway in the desert it would be impossible to buy, beg, borrow, or steal anything, so I had to think of every detail in advance. When the list was ready, I gave it to Ruby and said, "I'll be back in two weeks. I hope everything will be ready by then."

"It will be. You can count on us," Yohai said.

We said good-bye, and they left to go back to Jerusalem.

4

One by One

I left Beauty and Lightning in the hands of Naftali, an old friend of mine who lived in Hanegev. I took Dana with me, as well as my trusty pipe—which I never part with—and a little knapsack with a few things for the journey.

My first stop was at the agricultural school where Gil was studying. He was delighted to see me, but, as I expected, wouldn't show it. Only his eyes betrayed his feeling. He stroked Dana and whispered, "My lady, my lovely." She wagged her tail and pranced around him. Dana loved to play with Gil; sometimes they used to race each other. Dana could win, paws down, but the canny beast played it smart and held herself back, keeping only half a step ahead of him. It was a joy to watch them.

I spoke to the principal. It was almost vacation time anyway, and I was eager to take Gil with me. I had always meant to steel him against danger and knew that there is no substitute for experience in developing a man's courage, honor, and endurance. The principal wasn't too happy about my suggestion, since Gil's class hadn't finished its exams. But I promised that Gil would take them when he returned. The principal finally came around, and wished us a successful journey.

Gil was excited when I told him about the expedition. For reasons of safety I had decided not to tell any of the participants what our real purpose was. The less they knew about it—until the time came—the better the chances of carrying it off successfully.

"This is great, Father," Gil said. "I'm sick of sitting around and studying. It's about time I did something interesting."

"I thought you were interested in your studies." I said.

"I am. But I miss Dana. And I've been dying to see Lightning. And . . . " He fumbled for a moment. "I've missed you. A lot."

We were both silent. We knew how we felt about each other, and there was no need to talk about it. Gil went to pack his things, and we were on our way. We were going to see the first recruit for our party, my old friend Zevulun, whom we called "Zr'ir." We had been friends since the days we stood guard together in Galilee and had shared our work, our dreams, our adventures.

Zevulun lived in a little village in Judea. He worked as a watchman but also farmed a plot of land on which he had planted an orchard and a vineyard. Zevulun was a giant of a man, with an enormous moustache bristling in the midst of his flushed, smiling face. His body was massive, and he had powerful muscles. He needed an especially sturdy horse because of his weight. "Zr'ir" means

"Peewee" in Arabic. The Arabs had nicknamed him that, for fun.

Zevulun was a faithful friend, easygoing, and ready for anything. He was always bubbling over with good humor, always jolly and game, able to wave away minor difficulties with a flourish of his massive hand and to solve real problems without fuss.

The little house was surrounded by greenery. A creeper with blue flowers clung to its walls. A hedge ran around the property. I pushed open the little yellow gate, and the three of us—Dana, Gil and I—walked in. The courtyard was clean and neat; one saw the hand of a skilled housewife. Yocheved, Zevulun's wife, looked after it.

"Yirmi!" She cried from the porch at the back. "Can it really be you? It's been years! And this is Gil, right? Come here, you rascal! Do you remember how I used to hold you in my arms and tell you stories?"

"I don't remember," Gil muttered, blushing to the roots of his hair.

"It doesn't matter," Yocheved said, and settled us in chairs on the porch. Then she hurried to get a little basket of red-cheeked plums and bright green grapes, and before we knew it a pitcher of cold water was standing on the table, with a jug of fruit juice and heavy glasses beside it. She moved briskly, quietly, and energetically.

"Drink up," she said. "Water restores the soul. And the juice is freshly squeezed."

We sat on the porch. It was very pleasant. Yocheved bustled about, looking after us, chattering all the time about the latest news in our circle. One Guardsman, thank God, had married and gone into farming; another had been shot; a third had had a son; and so forth and so on.

We were still sitting and gossiping when a horseman on a tall, brown mare rode through the gate. Zevulun-Zr'ir and his horse, Dinah, stood in the yard. Zevulun had hardly changed, except for a touch of gray in his hair and moustache.

"Hey, Yocheved!" he called. "Isn't there any cold water in this house anymore?"

"There is, there is," she said, and winked at us. "Let's see how he greets you."

Zevulun tied his horse to the post in the yard. We heard his heavy steps on the stairs. He opened the door, strode through the house, and came out on the porch. He stooped slightly to get through the doorway, straightened up, stood still for a moment, and then fixed his eyes on me and shouted: *"Ahlan W'sahlan*—Welcome, Yirmi, you son of a gun!" He ran toward me, gave me a bear hug—Arab style—and slapped my back till he practically broke it.

"And this is Gil?" he cried. "Come here son," he said, and swung the boy into the air. "And Dana? Come here, you rascal," he roared and tried to pet her, but a fierce growl checked him.

"So, Yirmi. What's up? Tell me. It's been years, you son of a she-wolf! You've gone and stuck yourself in a god-forsaken hole in the Negev! We never see that ugly mug of yours anymore!"

"And how are you?" I asked.

"Al hamdu-lillah—thank God," he replied. "Life goes on. Everything finds its level. But there's no weeping, no wailing. Sometimes you're in the saddle, sometimes in the fields. One day it's honey, the next, vinegar, as our Arab friends say.

"Yocheved!" he called to his wife. "Have they eaten?"

"Not yet."

"Good God! Not eaten! No matter, though. You'll eat, Zevulun's way—till you burst. Come," he said to his wife. "I'll give you a hand."

Zevulun was a master at preparing Arab dishes—luscious, hot, and tangy. In the old days, when we were at a farm in Galilee, we sometimes used to make him cook for us, and he always saw to it that we ate and drank of the best.

Zevulun put on a white apron and went into the kitchen to help his wife. The table was covered by an embroidered white tablecloth, and soon, one after another, there appeared sizzling hot onion omelets, a salad made of tomatoes, cucumbers, scallions, peppers, chunks of white radish, and spicy green olives; a dish of fine sour cream; slabs of sweet white cheese and a kind of salty goat's cheese called *brindza;* a great loaf of black bread, dusted with white flour; a brick of sweet butter; and a huge pitcher of fruit juice.

Yocheved brought big earthenware plates, and dished out food for us. Zevulun opened a bottle of wine, and cried, "What about some of this red, red stuff, Yirmi? Shall we have a sip?"

He poured the wine, and we drank to all our old comrades, now scattered over the land.

"It warms your innards—eh, Yirmi? It's a real underground weapon, this wine. Before you know it, it's worked its way through you and goes to your head."

We ate heartily, our silence punctuated by occasional urgings from our host: "Taste this!" "Try that!" He picked and chose among the dishes, dropping the choicest bits on my plate and Gil's.

We finished the wine, which did its work rapidly. Zevulun grew jolly and talkative. When we could eat no more, Zevulun brewed spicy Arab coffee, with fragrant grains of *hel* floating in it. We sipped the coffee. Then I lit my pipe, and Zevulun took a cigarette.

We sat back, satisfied and silent.

It was time to get down to business. I knew that Zevulun would not need much urging. He always warmed to adventure. Nor was I mistaken. But Yocheved's pleading eyes betrayed displeasure. During her long life with Zevulun, she had suffered much from their prolonged separations, from the long, lonely nights when he had been away on watch somewhere.

The couple had no children. Zevulun loved children, and when we were single he used to talk about how he would raise his son. He had always been sure that if he had a child, it would be a son, and he knew that he would teach him to ride horses, shoot guns, and be brave and honest—in short, to be a man. But his dream had never come true.

"Listen, Zevulun," I said. "I can't tell you exactly what we're aiming at, but believe me, it's very important. And I need people like you."

"O.K. I'll go," he answered.

"Zevulun," Yocheved said. "Another one of your long journeys . . . " Tears glistened in her eyes.

"Listen, my dear," Zevulun said, softly. "I'll ask my brother to come and stay with you while I'm away. He'll be glad to visit here for a couple of weeks. My brother in Haifa," he said, turning to me, "who deals in dried fruit. He's not very busy now, since the season hasn't started. He'll be glad to come."

We sat up late that night, telling tales of the old times for Gil's benefit. But finally we went to sleep on fresh

34

linens laid out for us by Yocheved. I was pleased. We were four treasure-hunters now: Zevulun, Gil, Dana, and I.

In the morning we said good-bye to Yocheved, Zevulun, and Dinah, the brown mare. Zevulun had decided to transport Dinah to the Negev by train, to save time, so that he wouldn't have to be away from home longer than was absolutely necessary.

Our next stop was at Ein Harod, a kibbutz in the Valley of Jezreel, where my friend Jezreeli lived. He had been shot years back while standing guard, and the bullet had smashed the bones of his lower left arm. The doctor had had to amputate, almost to the elbow. But Jezreeli managed, somehow, to do the work of two hands with one. He could ride a horse and shoot a gun, using his bad arm in an auxiliary way. Since he had left the Guards, Jezreeli had become a machinist, working his lathe with "a hand and a half," as he used to say.

Jezreeli had joined a kibbutz. He had married—his wife's name was Shoshana—and he had a lovely daughter called Herut and a two-year-old son named Boaz. I had never seen the boy, having in fact heard of his birth only recently from a mutual Bedouin friend who travels around the countryside.

Gil, Dana, and I followed the road leading to the kibbutz, where we immediately made our way to the machine shop. My friend stood behind his lathe, turning a long steel rod. A sliver of steel curled off the axle and dangled to the floor. We stood watching as Jezreeli oiled the lathe. At last the sliver snapped and fell onto the pile of metal shavings on the floor. Jezreeli stopped the lathe. He looked up and saw us.

His face, ordinarily serious, lit up with a smile. He quietly shook my hand, then Gil's, and patted Dana on the back.

Jezreeli was a man of few words. He was renowned for his even temper and imperturbable calm. He never showed anger or dismay. And he strove to be logical about everything.

There were many stories about Jezreeli's "cool." I had told Gil one of them on our way to Ein Herod. One night Jezreeli had been on duty, without a horse. It was a moonlit night, and he had been walking along a path that wound its way through a field of standing corn. Suddenly a pair of riders appeared, one on a dark horse, the other on a white one. Both of them had come to a stop some distance from him. One of them called out. "Do you have a cigarette?"

Jezreeli knew they meant trouble. He unslung his rifle, cocked it, and fell to the ground in the field.

"I don't smoke," he answered.

"Then give us a light," the voice replied.

Such a request, at such an hour, could mean nothing good: probably robbery, possibly murder. Jezreeli answered calmly, "The cigarette is stuck in the mouth of my gun. Come, my master, and light it." It was a common rejoinder among the Bedouin of the region.

The riders spurred their horses and galloped toward Jezreeli. But it was difficult to aim from the saddle, and their target was hidden in the corn. Jezreeli carefully sighted the white horse, clearly visible in the darkness, and shot. The horse whinnied with pain, and reared. It threw its rider and galloped away into the night. The second horseman dismounted, and the two men, leading the dark horse, stumbled off in the direction they had come from. Jezreeli got up and continued making his rounds. He woke no one and told no one of the encounter. The next morning it was learned that a white mare belonging to the *mukhtar* of the nearby Circassian village had been shot during the night.

Jezreeli was a devoted friend. You could always rely on him under fire. We'd been on many missions together. He'd saved my life more than once and solved problems that had seemed insoluble. He had kindly blue eyes, and a dark, somewhat angular face. His right arm was muscular and powerful, and his fingers were deft and nimble. He used to carve in wood with a simple shoemaker's knife, in his spare time. He had made several statues, each of them a work of art.

It was noon. The lunch bell sounded from the communal dining hall. Members of the big settlement, in their work clothes, streamed into the building.

"Come," Jezreeli said, inviting us to join them.

On the way to the dining room I asked him about Halo, his mare, to whom he was very attached.

"She's in the kibbutz stable," he said. "When I joined the settlement, I put her in the communal herd. But now I look after her myself."

In the dining room I shook hands with many members of the settlement whom I'd known for years. Some of them knew Gil and even Dana. By the time we reached our table, my hand ached from all the handshaking. Meanwhile, Shoshana, Jezreeli's wife, had come in, and we sat down at the table together.

When the meal was over, our host took us to the children's house to see his son, Boaz, who was playing out-of-doors in a wooden playpen. He was a sturdy, sunburnt little boy, with blue eyes like his father's. He was delighted to have Dana come up to him and fearlessly stretched out his hand to pet her.

"When he grows up, he'll make a stalwart guardsman," I said to Jezreeli.

Herut, Jezreeli's five-year-old daughter, joined us, in blue pants and a white shirt, with heavy braids hanging over her shoulders. She remembered me and talked about Ronit, the doll I had brought her on one of my visits.

Finally, when we were sitting in Jezreeli's room, I brought up my proposal, without mentioning the Pasha's treasure. Jezreeli thought for a while, and said, "All right, I'll come. I'm starting my vacation, anyhow. While you're recruiting the rest of our party, I'll take Halo and pay some visits I owe to my Bedouin friends. But I'll meet you at your house in good time."

Shoshana made no objections. She knew that once her husband had made up his mind, nothing could get him to change it. It wouldn't matter if she "stood on her head and wagged her tail," as she used to say to tease him.

I was glad Jezreeli had agreed to come. Things would be easier with him along. He was a crack shot, skillful with pistol and dagger, and his head was full of clever schemes and strategies. Where his weapons couldn't get him out of a jam, his good sense would.

That night we stayed in Jezreeli's modest room, which was like the rooms all the members of the settlement lived in, and early next morning we started out.

There were five of us now.

Our next stop was at Hasson and Na'amah's. We got

off the bus in the foothills of the Carmel Mountains. A winding path led up to Hasson's house. We walked along the path, and I told Gil about Hasson and his wife, both of whom came from old Jewish families in the Caucasus.

Hasson was a tall, slender man, with black eyes and black eyebrows, dark skin, coal-black hair, and an elegant black moustache. He was a son of the East to his fingertips. Descended from a tribe of fighting Jews, he had been reared in the traditions of the Orient: blood vengeance, hospitality, friendship unto death, and boundless loyalty to family and tribe. Hasson was a man of his word; he would not go back on a promise if it cost him his life, and he found the least breach of justice incomprehensible. He and his wife, Na'amah, had been engaged to each other when they were still children. Hasson was a veteran Guardsman, known and venerated by Arab and Bedouin alike. We had been Guards together in one of the villages of Lower Galilee.

Hasson had come to Palestine in the early days, with his mother and his younger brother, who had also joined the Guards. Hasson's mother was a vigorous old woman, strong and straight as an oak tree, and she did her work with an agility remarkable in someone her age. She baked Arab bread in a *tabun*—the simple earthen oven that Arab women used. But she also knew how to dress a freshly slaughtered beast, to clean her men's guns, and—when the need arose—to shoot with deadly accuracy. Her tradition gave women an honored place at their husband's side, which was rare among the peoples of the East.

Hasson and Na'amah lived in a little stone house at the edge of a forest. For some time now Hasson had been working as a guard on behalf of the National Forest

Association, looking after its forests on the Carmel. Before he came, local villagers had made serious inroads on the plantings; they felled trees, devastated nurseries and poachers burned healthy trees to make charcoal. Hasson had put a stop to that, and in doing so had come to be both feared and respected among them.

Hasson's sons helped him in his work. Gilad, the elder, was about seventeen, and Yoram—who had been named for Hasson's younger brother—about ten. In time of need Na'amah could ride a horse and shoot a gun like a man; and little Yoram was already a fair marksman. Their house was isolated and exposed, and every available gun-hand was needed in case of a raid. The little stone house also served as the family fortress; from it, they could hold off any attack by marauders.

We drew near the house. Queenie, Hasson's mare, was grazing in the yard. Hasson's sons were hoeing the garden, and Na'amah was feeding the chickens, who flocked around her with clucking glee. They pecked seeds on the ground and sometimes jabbed at Na'amah's feet. She would scream comically and then laugh.

"Hello, Yirmi," Na'amah cried, and scattered an apronful of chicken feed among the fowl. She hurried toward me and shook my hand.

"Hasson," she called. "Hasson—we have a guest!"

Hasson came out of the house and hurried toward us. He led us inside and invited us to sit in the *madafa*—the guest room, which was furnished in Middle Eastern style, with low divans, embroidered cushions, colorful carpets, and beaten brass trays with little coffee cups on them. Antique rifles, pistols, and swords hung on the walls, and *hookahs*, with long coiled pipes and little amber mouthpieces, stood on the floor waiting to be smoked.

40

We sat in a little circle, reclining on colorful pillows and sipping our coffee. Hasson told me about their life in the house on the Carmel, which they called "The Abode of Strength." He spoke slowly, with oriental calm. He knew all the customs and rituals of the desert nomads and had adopted their way of speaking.

When the boys had gone to sleep, I told Hasson about our mission. He immediately agreed to join us. Gilad, his elder son, was old enough to patrol the forest for a while. The area had quieted down of late. The prowlers had moved on to places where it was easier to ply their trade, so Gilad would be able to look after the forest alone.

"Zevulun and Jezreeli will also join us," I said.

"Ai, ai, ai." Hasson sighed with pleasure. "We'll be together again, as in the old days. 'Old wine is good wine,' as they say. Together, we can do anything. Our experience is worth the strength of twenty young men. 'Years nurture wisdom, and experience nourishes understanding.'"

Breakfast was ready when I got up the next morning: hot milk, tasty omelets, fresh bread, and butter.

"Fresh greens are better than the fatted calf," Hasson said. "We don't eat meat in this house because of the cost, but vegetables, eggs, and milk—*al hamdu-lillah*—we have in plenty."

We ate and bade the Hasson family farewell. Then we headed for the road to Lower Galilee.

Our party had found its sixth member. Now for the seventh.

After traveling a good while, we caught a glimpse of the Sea of Galilee, which we call the Kinneret. It lay there below us, blue and shimmering, like a great mirror, with violet hills surrounding it. I am always moved when I see the Kinneret, with the memories it brings back of my early days in Galilee.

"And where are we going now, Father?" Gil asked.

"There are two more people who I hope will join us," I replied. "The first of them is a very strange man. He is called Yisrael the Shepherd, but we always call him 'The Dreamer.' He is a vegetarian and a naturalist, and his head is filled with ideas of the simple life, the life of nature. He thinks we have a unique destiny in the history of mankind, and especially in the Middle East. He believes that as Jews, we should be nomads, that we should live in tents like the Bedouin, dress like them, and—like them—be masters of gun and steed. Or else we should live like simple peasants, with few needs, satisfied with what the land yields and beasts provide.

"Srulik, as we used to call him, was an excellent watchman. When he first joined the Guards, he went to live among the Bedouin, learned their customs and their ways with sheep and cattle. He speaks marvelous Arabic, like a real son of the desert.

"One day, a group of us were sitting together under a tree on a farm in Lower Galilee. It was afternoon, and we were cleaning our guns, preparing for the evening's watch. Suddenly a Bedouin horseman appeared, mounted on a fine mare, such as I have rarely seen. He drew near, and we saw that he was armed with a rifle, pistol, and dagger. He stopped and greeted us. That is the Bedouin custom: The rider defers to the pedestrian, as a matter of courtesy, and greets him first.

"'Marhabara,' he said—'Blessings upon you.'"

"'Marhabtain,' we replied—'And upon you. Dismount, and enjoy the shade of our tree. We will bring you water to drink and coffee, if you wish it.' 'With pleasure,' the Bedouin replied. 'I am weary with travel.'

"The stranger dismounted and sat under the tree, We brought him water and coffee, and he thanked us in honey-tongued Arabic. Then he asked about our affairs—how so-and-so was doing, how such-and-such was feeling. We were amazed. This stranger knew all about us, even the names of our wives and children! How could that be?

"We sat, eyeing him suspiciously, until our guest removed his headdress. 'You still don't know who I am?' he asked.

"It took a moment before we recognized him. It was Srulik, the Shepherd—our Yisrael, the Dreamer. Even his mother would not have known him."

We passed Kiryat Shmuel, a suburb of Tiberias, and reached the lower city, on the shores of the Sea. Getting off the bus, we were surrounded with vendors hawking their wares—*tamarhindi*, a sweetish drink, *baklava*, its paper thin pastry dripping with honey and flower seeds and pistachios, Indian nuts and coffee. Each vendor praised his own goods and disparaged those of his neighbors. They fought desperately for every penny we might spend until Dana bared her teeth and fangs and scared them away.

I bought two portions of *falafel*—a hot chick-pea delicacy. The vendor split a cake of flat Arab bread, popped the fragrant golden balls of *falafel* into it, added pickles and tomato segments, poured sesame oil over them, and sprinkled *sehug*—pickled hot pepper—on top.

I shouldered my knapsack, and munching our *falafel*, we walked along the banks of the Sea, passing houses built of basalt, the gray-black, volcanic rock of the region, and great bushes laden with red flowers that looked like tongues of flame and gave off a spicy scent.

We passed avenues of tall eucalyptus, between whose heavy boughs we caught glimpses of the Kinneret—glimmering, cool, and inviting. We found a sheltered spot, stripped, and jumped into the water. Gil swam incredibly fast; I couldn't keep up with him. Dana also jumped in and swam along with Gil. I returned to shore, and watched the boy's lithe body cutting through the water with bold, broad strokes, as Dana's head moved smoothly behind him, lying flat on the rippling deep.

Gil returned and climbed out of the water. Dana shook herself dry, flashing waterdrops in every direction. It was a lovely day, and the surroundings were stunning. I began to sing, and Gil joined in, with his fresh and vibrant voice. Dana, who seemed pleased with our singing, opened her mouth and barked gaily. She capered around us as we walked, hurrying to overtake us after she had lagged behind or chased mice to their holes.

At last we came on Srulik the Dreamer's little paradise. He had found himself a charming stretch of rich black loam, between the lake and the mountains. It was crossed by a small aqueduct that carried water from a mountainside spring. The water flowed through a concrete pool that Srulik had built, into irrigation ditches that watered the place.

His land was beautifully cultivated. He had planted a little vineyard on part of it, where clusters of early grapes were already ripening. Elsewhere he had planted fruit trees: golden apricots, red-blossoming pomegranates, apples, pears, almonds, dates, and citrus. There were also herb and flower gardens, with fragrant beds of spices and medicinal herbs.

The house was covered with vines. A creeper, bearing blue flowers with yellow centers, climbed up the western wall. A long, narrow porch ran the length of the northern side, shaded by a vine burdened with dark purple grapes. Rose bushes and red carnations surrounded the house. The sweet scent of jasmine was everywhere. Barns and stables stood on the eastern part of the farm. Water flowed through little open canals, purling along as it irrigated the garden.

"Father, it's like paradise!" Gil cried, amazed at the loveliness around him.

"Right," I said. "That's what we used to call it: heaven on earth! This is what you get when you combine hard work with love of the soil and respect for its produce."

We found Srulik in his house. He was having lunch. He seemed the dreamer he had always been: the same kindly eyes, the same warm but bashful smile at the corners of his mouth.

Srulik was obviously pleased to see us and immediately sat us on the porch, brought us a bowl of cold water to wash in, and left us to rest while he got us something to eat.

We sat looking at the blue lake beyond the trees and flowers. Mt. Arbel, which was known as "The Mountain of the Zealots," loomed opposite us.

Srulik brought a little table and placed it before us. On it he set a huge bowl of salad and vegetables, a basket of fresh fruit, jugs of various juices, little plates with herbs and spices, and a bowl of amber-colored honey.

We ate the food prepared for us by our vegetarian host,

and it was delicious; we didn't miss the meat, the bread, and the coffee to which we were accustomed. And Dana enjoyed the leftovers.

After lunch our host took us on a tour of his grounds. First we visited his thoroughbred horse, Lord. He was of an English breed, handsome and tall, with a glossy brown coat, an arched neck, close-cropped mane, and wise eyes. Srulik was more attached to Lord than he was to any other being, man or beast. Then Srulik took us to a grassy stretch of the lake shore. Here the water was so clear we could see the white sand and the glistening shells at the bottom of the lake.

"This is my 'swimming hole'," he said. "I bathe here every day, summer and winter."

All of us stripped and dove into the water. Even though he was already middle-aged, Srulik was as lean and sinewy as a man half his age—suntanned, taut, and supple. His wiry body bespoke both power and endurance. In the course of his lifetime he had done a great deal of traveling in Palestine and the neighboring countries. He sometimes used to talk about his life as a shepherd among Bedouin and about his wanderings in the Arabian desert. It was said he had even visited Mecca, disguised as a son of the desert. But he wouldn't talk about that—probably because he had sworn secrecy to the sheikh who had smuggled him in.

When we went back to the house, Ahmed Muhamad abu-Talal joined us. Ahmed was an Arab friend of Srulik from his shepherd days among the Bedouin. In those days Srulik had dreamed of a great Mediterranean commonwealth where Jews and Arabs could live together in harmony and peace. Yet when the Arabs attacked the

Jews, he had fought like a lion. Ahmed lived in a Bedouin tent on Srulik's property, and Talal, his son, lived with him, together with his family, which included the young man's wives, Gamila and Sa'ada. Srulik and Ahmed worked the land together and lived in peace and friendship, even in times of trouble.

The time passed in conversation. Ahmed fingered the beads of his *mazbeha*—the string of beads on which pious Moslems "tell" their prayers. When evening began to fall, Ahmed got up, blessed us, and returned to his tent. Then I told Srulik the reason for my coming and invited him to join our expedition.

Srulik thought for a moment, and said, "The truth is, I had decided to give up adventure, horses, and travel. I want to live on my land and enjoy the fruit of my labors. But I can't turn an old friend down, and I understand that it is an important matter. So I'll come. I'll leave my place in Ahmed's hands, take Lord, and come with you."

Srulik sighed and continued, "I once hoped that many people would come here, and that we would live together in clans and tribes, like the Bedouin—that we would live a simple life, rooted in the soil, like our ancestors in biblical times. But my dream was only a dream; all my friends have gone their ways and left me to my dreams." He was silent for a moment and then he added, "But look, Yirmi. Here, on my own land, I live as I like. I have made the world I dreamed of."

5

In the House of Isma'in al-Atrash

In the morning, Srulik sent us on our way, having promised to be at my house on the appointed day, riding Lord, his stallion.

We headed for the road leading northward to Upper Galilee. I had spent much time as a Guard in the far-flung settlements in Upper Galilee, among its mountains, its jutting crags, its winding paths, and its hidden villages. My good friend, Isma'in al-Atrash, the Hunter, lived in one of those Druze villages.

We stood at the roadside and tried to thumb a ride. Many drivers passed us without even bothering to signal that they had no room. But finally a big truck pulled up. Its driver was an Arab who was going to the village of Halsa in Upper Galilee. Gil handed Dana to me, and I made her comfortable on a sack. The driver started the truck, and we began to climb the road that led to the north. It commanded a wonderful view of the inland sea. We watched the shifting sweep of the lake, and Gil asked me to tell him about Isma'in the Hunter.

"As you know," I said, "there are Druze in Lebanon and Palestine, but most of them live in Syria, in the Jebel Druze—the Druze mountains. During 1925 and 1926, the Druze staged a massive uprising against the French, who were already ruling Syria at the time. It was a guerrilla war. The Druze would swoop down on the French, ambush them, and cut their supply lines.

"I was in the Jebel Druze on a secret mission for the Guards. I was staying at an inn in a Druze village at a time when there was heavy fighting in the region. The French had brought up their artillery, and were bombarding the mountain villages.

"One morning I woke up early and went to see how my mare, Lady, was doing. Suddenly, a little gate opened, and a young Druze came rushing into the courtyard. He carried a rifle. Two cartridge belts were slung across his chest, and there was a pistol in his holster. He had been shot in the hand and was bleeding profusely. His clothes were stained with blood, and he left a bloody trail behind him. I recalled that I had heard shooting a few minutes before and assumed that the young man had been hit in the exchange.

" 'In the name of merciful Allah,' he cried. 'Give me sanctuary!'

"He was relying on an old Bedouin custom, which the Druze and even the village Arabs observed. A man fleeing the *joom*—that is, the dreadful law of blood vengeance— or pursued by any enemy could enter a house and say, 'I seek sanctuary, under God and in the shadow of this house,' and the owner was obliged to protect him.

" 'I am not the master of this house,' I said.

" 'I stand in the shadow of your mercy, courageous one!' the young man replied.

" 'The French are close on my heels,' he went on. 'They shot my horse out from under me, and now they seek my life. They will be here in a minute!'

"He was obviously a courageous young man. I couldn't refuse him protection. I quickly led him behind the stable, to a tall haystack in which I dug a hole. I helped him into it and covered him over with hay. 'Don't move,' I said. 'The slightest movement can cost your life.' 'Blessings upon you,' he replied. 'You are a good man.'

"I took a broom and covered his tracks with horse droppings strewn around the courtyard. Then I took my horse out of the stable and stood her alongside the haystack, to browse.

"I was still bustling about when a troop of horsemen came galloping into the courtyard. A tall sergeant with a heavy moustache led them, rifle in hand.

" '*Sabah al heir*,' I called, in Arabic: 'Good morning, sergeant.' '*Sabah al nur*,' he replied. 'Have you seen a wounded Druze around?' 'No,' I said. 'My eyes have seen no wounded Druze.' 'Damn the son of a mongrel dog!' he said. He thought I was an Arab, since I was wearing native robes and the native headdress.

" 'We've almost caught Isma'in al-Atrash,' the sergeant said. 'The treacherous dog leads a band of upstart Druze, and he's made no end of trouble.'

" 'Really?' I said.

" 'We got his horse and seem to have hit him as well, but he's disappeared. He's left a trail of blood, and it leads to the gate of this inn.'

" 'I've seen no one,' I replied.

" 'Search the inn,' the sergeant commanded. His horsemen dismounted and began to search the courtyard. One of them walked up to the haystack, and stuck his bayonet into it. But the sight of the horse peacefully chewing her hay convinced him no one was there.

" 'No one here!' the sergeant said. 'I know it, sergeant,' I said. 'We've seen no one this morning.'

"The sergeant called his soldiers together, and they left. The moment they were gone, I dug the fugitive out of the haystack, brought cold water, and washed his wound. It was fortunately only a flesh wound. I dressed it and then brought him bread and milk. He rained a thousand grateful blessings on my head.

"After I had led him to the gate, he turned to me and said, 'My name is Isma'in al-Atrash, the Hunter. I am from the village of Marar on the banks of the Hatzbani. My house is your house, my possessions your possessions; whatever I own is yours to enjoy. If you are in trouble, call on me. I am at your disposal, I and my rifle, my pistol, my sword. Ask, and you will learn that anyone who leans on Isma'in al-Atrash—on his rifle, his pistol, his sword—will know peace.'

"I wished Isma'in well. He turned, walked through the gate, and disappeared.

"I have often seen Isma'in since that day, in times of war and times of peace, and he has always kept his word. He has lent me his strong right arm—with his rifle, pistol, sword, and cunning—whenever I needed it. Isma'in is a master huntsman, who pursues the bear, the boar, the gazelle, and the hare in the snow-capped mountains of Lebanon. He has an uncanny instinct for finding his way in the trackless wilds of the region. He will reach his destination in unknown terrain on a moonless night and never go astray. He carries salt, matches, and a hunting knife wherever he goes and can live on his catch for great lengths of time and travel great distances without looking to man for nourishment."

I was still telling Gil about Isma'in when the truck passed Rosh Pina and reached the customs house, where armed soldiers check vehicles coming from Syria on the Damascus-Rosh Pina road.

The truck stopped near a store run by an old woman named Gittel, whom everyone called Grandma Gittel. Arab bandits had burned her shop and killed her only son. But the old woman would not give up, and stayed on, rebuilding her store and serving her customers. I knew her from the old days.

We got out, and after greeting Gittel, ate and drank our fill, and having fed Dana, climbed back onto the truck and continued our journey northward. We passed the intersection of the road to Mahanaim and Damascus, the settlement of Ayelet Hashahar, the road leading to Yisud Ham'alah, and finally reached the village of Halsa.

We climbed out of the truck, thanked the driver, and followed the trail that led to the village of Marar. Isma'in's house stood away from the other houses of the village. It was painted blue and surrounded by a garden in the center of which was a hut.

We were still looking around when we heard a horse whinnying. It was my good friend Isma'in riding toward us. He was returning from a hunt on his great horse Abyad—"the white one." Abyad was a handsome beast, with a smooth, glossy coat, a heavy mane that fell over both sides of his neck, a small head, great green eyes, broad nostrils, a powerful chest, a fine tail, and a muscular body.

Isma'in was now in middle-age. He was broad-backed

and sunburnt, with a heavy moustache and a youthful spark in his eye. His hunting rifle rested on his shoulder. His saddle was decorated with colorful mats, and he was followed by his bow-legged, spindle-waisted dog, who was matchless in the hunt.

The moment Isma'in saw me he sprang from his saddle and ran toward me, silver spurs jingling. He embraced me, kissed me on both cheeks, and cried, "So you've come, Shattar, my friend! I've not seen you in years. *Al hamdu-lillah*—praise be to God that you've honored me again, and come to rest in the shade of my roof."

Isma'in handed the reins of his horse to Suleiman, his eldest son, who had come out to meet him, and led us into the house. He hung his rifle on the wall and took off his boots and hunting clothes. Then he went into another room and returned with two bearskins for us to sit on. "I hunted these bears down, in the forests of Lebanon," he said.

Isma'in made coffee, and as we drank and chatted, visitors began to arrive. Isma'in was one of the village notables, and his house was the center of its social life.

Isma'in related how he had hunted bear, wild boar, and gazelle in various places, and invited us to join him on a bear hunt on Mount Lebanon. I indicated, however, that I had another, more serious proposal to make.

After we had eaten and belched to show we were satisfied, as is the custom among desert peoples, we sipped coffee and smoked hookahs or cigarettes. When the guests had left, I told Isma'in about the expedition to the Sinai desert.

"Anything you ask of me, Abu-Gil, my friend, I will do," Isma'in said. "A bond of blood-brotherhood joins us for-

ever. I will come with you and help you in every way
that I can."

In the morning I got up and went into the yard to
wash my face in cold water from the well. Mt. Hermon
glistened opposite me, covered with snow even in summer,
with verdant villages on its lower slopes. Breakfast was
ready: *pitah*, eggs, yoghurt, honey, and hot milk. We ate
a hearty breakfast, and then visited in the village with
Isma'in, and bathed in the icy waters of the Hatzbani. At
noon we returned to his house and prepared to leave.

Part II
The Treasure Hunt

6

The Journey Begins

When we got home, Beauty greeted me with an exuberant whinny, and Lightning laid his head on Gil's shoulder. Dana scampered about in the courtyard, barking wildly.

Our party began to assemble, and within a few days the entire company had arrived. The house echoed with Zevulun's thundering laughter and Hasson's storytelling.

One day a Bedouin appeared, leading a mule with two heavy sacks on its back.

"Does *Hawaja* Yirmi live here?" he asked.

"I am Yirmi," I replied.

"The mule is for you." he said.

"Hey, Yirmi!" Zevulun shouted. "What's the mule for? And the sacks? Have you become a smuggler in your old age?"

"Could be," I said, to avoid answering in the presence of a stranger. I gave the Bedouin a cup of coffee and a big glass of water, tipped him and sent him on his way.

It was a warm, early summer evening. We were all

sitting on my porch: Zevulun, whose chair chould hardly hold him, and creaked ominously; Hasson, whose white teeth gleamed in the dark; Jezreeli, with his earnest face; Srulik, lean and sinewy; Isma'in, my blood-brother, sitting on the floor in oriental fashion; Gil and I. I put Dana outside to keep watch, and I knew she would bark if a stranger approached.

"Well, Yirmi," Hasson challenged. "Open your mouth and speak. Why are we here?"

I was silent for a moment, waiting for everybody to become still.

"It is good to have so many friends from the old days in my house. Those were good times for all of us, and challenging ones. But now I have a new challenge—one that only all of us, pulling together, can meet."

"Two are always better than one, and a triple cord is even harder to snap," Hasson commented.

"Exactly. I still may not tell you our final destination. But first we must get to the monastery of St. Catherine in the Sinai desert."

"Well, well!" Zevulun cried, astonished. "That *is* a long way."

"Yes," I said. "A very long way. We will travel on horseback, with one pack mule for supplies. Each one of us must carry his own roll of blankets, canteen, food for himself, and fodder for his horse. I hope we will enjoy Bedouin hospitality on the way so that we can keep our own supplies for emergencies."

"What about firearms?" Jezreeli said. "The Sinai desert is full of bandits and warrior tribes. They will attack any unarmed party."

"Of course. We'll be heavily armed. Each of us will

take his pistol, his rifle, and his dagger. And plenty of ammunition. Is everything clear?"

"As clear as the sun at noon," Hasson said.

"Dana will come with us."

"Very good," said Hasson. "She's worth any two of us."

"And Gil is coming along."

"Hoo!" Hasson cried. "The lambs grow up into rams."

Gil, who was sitting at my side, blushed and squirmed uncomfortably.

"What will we wear?" Srulik asked.

"Riding pants and boots, Arab robes, and headdresses. We want to pass as a party of Bedouin. Our desert hosts won't ask questions. Their code of hospitality forbids that. Anything else?"

"Yes," said Hasson.

"What?"

"Aren't we going to drink to the success of our expedition?"

"I'm dying of thirst anyway," said Zevulun.

I laughed, went into the house, and got a bottle of whiskey and a tray of glasses. I poured a drink for everyone but Srulik and Gil, for whom I had brought some fruit juice. We lifted our glasses.

"To our desert band!" Hasson toasted.

"To a safe journey!" said Zevulun.

"And a successful one!" I added.

We sipped our drinks. Gil tasted mine, blushed, coughed, and nearly choked.

We got up before dawn the next morning. It was still dark and chilly, and the sky in the east was just beginning to pale. A column of horsemen emerged from my courtyard. I was at its head, riding Beauty, and wearing a wide desert robe with a *kefiyeh* muffling my face. Gil, mounted on Lightning, rode alongside me. Dana ran between us. Zevulun followed on his mare, Halo, and then came Srulik on Lord and Hasson on Queenie, with Isma'in bringing up the rear, mounted on Abyad and leading the pack mule, with the pair of sacks on its back.

In the pale light of dawn shadowy figures of horses and men could be seen. Occasionally the barrel of a rifle or the butt of a revolver glistened, and one heard the steady hoofbeats of our mounts. We rode southward. The path wound its way among hillocks and sand dunes.

I had decided that we would travel in the early hours from dawn till about ten and then rest during the hot forenoon and early afternoon, seeking shelter among the Bedouin or in camps we would set up ourselves. Then we would resume our journey at four and ride on till seven or eight in the evening.

The eastern sky brightened, and fiery flame illuminated the horizon. Then the sun rose. Long shadows of men on horseback stretched across the sands, pushing forward into the desert wastes. A giant dog bobbed along among them.

Slowly, it got hotter and hotter. Sand thrown by the horses' hooves shrouded the riders in a dense cloud. The horses sweated and the saddles stank. We rode along in silence for hours on end. Occasionally a bewildered rabbit would come scrambling between the horses' legs, a single deer would flit by among the dunes, or we would pass a doe with her fawn standing stock still under a tamarisk tree. The desert is not altogether desolate.

It was ten in the morning. We had seen no Bedouin encampments, and so we tethered the horses in the shade of broom trees and unsaddled them near some green shrubs they could nibble on. Then we opened our knapsacks and got ready to eat. Gil gathered dry branches and lit a campfire. I got the coffee pot, everyone poured a cupful of his water into it, and I put it on the fire to boil.

Isma'in mixed a little flour and water, kneaded the dough, and baked flat bread among the embers. We sat around the fire, ate, and drank hot coffee. Afterward, we got up, poured a little water into our cupped palms, and let the horses lick it. We planned to reach a watering place by evening, where the horses could drink their fill.

We unrolled our blankets, lay down in a shady spot, and dropped off to sleep. Each of us stood an hour's watch while the others slept.

In the afternoon we got up, packed our knapsacks, saddled the horses, and continued on our way.

We reached the water hole in the early evening. Arab boys were watering their flocks and filling rusty cans with water. We unsaddled the horses, waited for them to cool off, and asked one of the Bedouin to fill the drinking troughs so that the horses could drink. The appearance of an armed band with muffled faces squelched the chatter of the shepherds. They watched us, wide-eyed. We knew

they would return to their encampment with word of our arrival.

After the horses had had their fill of water, we drank and washed our sweaty faces. Then we saddled the horses again and rode on. It was already growing dark. From afar we saw a line of black tents pitched on a broad camping ground under a hillside. The sheikh was waiting for us and invited us to be his guests.

His boys took the horses and led them to be fed. The sheikh ushered us into his tent. He lived in a *muchamas*—a tent pitched on five poles—which meant that he was rich and powerful. We took off our shoes and sat down cross-legged, in a half-circle, with the sheikh in the middle. His boys brought pillows for us to lean on. The ritual of coffee-making began. Meanwhile, the notables of the tribe arrived, eager to hear what news we might bring from the great world outside.

We sipped the coffee and talked, never referring to the business we were on nor inquiring into our hosts' affairs. We knew that no questions would be asked of us. The Bedouin will entertain a passerby for three and a third days, during which time custom forbids him to question his guest.

The sheikh served us a meal of camel yoghurt, *burghul* —ground, cooked wheat—and fresh Arab bread baked by his wives.

When we had finished eating, each of us belched loudly to show that we had eaten enough. Afterwards, we sat around talking about weapons, horses, and desert lore.

Late that night, when the sheikh noticed our suppressed yawns, he ordered his boys to bring pillows and blankets and make up our pallets. Then we slept. The first day of our journey had passed without incident.

7

Heat

Day followed day. We rode mornings and evenings, rested during the heat of the day, and visited with the Bedouin we met. When we met none of these desert nomads, Isma'in hunted some beast and roasted the meat over an open fire. Srulik foraged for plants we could eat, and for those that stored moisture to quench our thirst. He found a plant that tasted like tea when steeped in boiling water and another that tasted like lettuce. It seemed that nothing escaped him. Sometimes he jumped off his horse as we rode along, picked a handful of plants, and put them in the bag that he had tied to his saddle. In the evening, he sorted out his finds and prepared the greens for dinner.

We advanced into the desert. We had already crossed the Palestinian border and had entered the Sinai. There we made our way over trails where the horses sank hoof-deep into the sand, or through flatlands covered with flinty stones. These stones could pierce a horse's hoof, and we had to make sure the horses were properly shod. I had brought along a heavy mallet, nails, and spare horseshoes. Jezreeli was in charge of the shoeing, managing the difficult task with his one hand.

We met fewer and fewer Bedouin as we moved deeper into Sinai and depended more and more on Isma'in's hunting and the plants that Srulik found.

On the eighth day we found ourselves climbing a steep mountain trail, with a sheer cliff on our left and the rocky mountainside so close on our right that our legs brushed against it as we rode.

Heat poured down in waves from above, and the rocks below reflected the sun's blinding light. There was no trace of shade in sight. Dana followed my horse, her tongue hanging out, panting with the heat. Beauty stumbled along heavily. It was already unbearably hot an hour after sunrise. The torrid desert wind was dry and oppressive. We would have stopped to rest at ten but had found no shade. We decided to plod on; it seemed better to keep moving than to sit still in the heat.

At noon we found a tamarisk clinging to a rocky hillside. We pulled up alongside it and dismounted with difficulty. The horses' ribs were heaving, and we unsaddled them. Each of us poured a little water into his palm and let his mount lap it up. I gave Dana a little water to drink. Gil helped me. His face was pale and tired, and heavy beads of sweat ran down his brow, but he didn't complain. Lightning was bathed in sweat. Sometimes he raised his head and neighed wearily. Dinah, Zevulun's powerful mare, rubbed her head against the trunk of the tamarisk. As Zevulun removed her saddle, sweat streamed down his neck, drenching his clothes.

Srulik, Jezreeli, and Isma'in, who were less affected by

the heat, lifted the saddles off their horses backs and prepared our lunch.

My limbs were heavy and my eyes smarted from weariness. We huddled in the shade of the tamarisk, ate our last food, and sipped almost all of our remaining water. Then we stretched out, crowding our heads into the shade of our saddles and abandoning our bodies to the burning sun.

The sun began to move westward. These were the hottest hours. Nothing stirred; we saw no living thing. Even the birds of prey had found some shelter from the searing sun.

In the afternoon, the sun began to slip behind the mountains, but the heat did not abate. We got up slowly and saddled our horses. We had decided not to ride them but to lead them on foot. We hung our rifles on the saddles to lighten our loads.

The path climbed to the mountain top and began to descend through a sloping canyon into a big valley surrounded by high granite mountains. We climbed down cautiously lest the horses stumble and break a leg. Isma'in had spotted signs of vegetation from the mountain top and so we hoped there would be water in the valley below.

We advanced at a snail's pace until we reached the valley. The horses were exhausted; their muscles quivered under their sweating hides. We decided to make camp, though the old map I carried indicated no water holes.

Srulik foraged among the rocks and found some strange-looking plants, which we chewed. They contained enough moisture to allay our thirst but left an unpleasant after taste.

The horses stood quietly by some bushes. They were very thirsty, but they didn't even try to munch the leaves.

We sat in silence. There was no point in lighting a fire, since there was no water to boil. And there was no food.

"If we don't find water tomorrow . . . " Zevulun said.

". . . we'll be in bad trouble," Hasson concluded.

"The horses won't get through another day like this," Srulik added.

Again we fell silent. There was no point in talking. I spread my blanket and Gil lay down alongside me. Dana lay between us, breathing heavily, sticking her tongue out to cool herself off.

I looked at the sky. It was full of brilliant stars. The valley was quiet. No light glimmered anywhere; there was no sign of a Bedouin tent.

I fell asleep thinking strange and disquieting thoughts and woke when it was still dark. My mouth was dry, and my pulse throbbed slowly because of my thirst. I lay on the blanket and thought over the situation. Finally I decided to wake Isma'in.

"Get up, Isma'in," I said.

He opened his eyes, sat up and asked, "Is that you, Abu-Gil?"

"We're in bad trouble," I said.

"I know, Abu-Gil."

"What do you think we should do?"

"There must be water holes somewhere in this valley," he said. "We've seen tall shrubs. That means there must be occasional floods. The entire valley is one big *wadi,* and sometimes it must be flooded."

"Well?"

"If there are floods, there must be water. But I don't know how to find it."

The night passed slowly, but finally morning approached. The fierce heat subsided and the pre-dawn coolness brought relief to our bodies.

"Listen!" said Isma'in. "I just remembered something! Yesterday, as we were climbing down into the valley, I saw fresh camel dung on the trail. That means a caravan passed here recently—merchants or narcotics smugglers on their way from Jordan to Egypt. Such people know where to find water, and they tend to camp alongside it. I also saw a bird that is found only where there is water. There has to be water somewhere in this valley. We'll let the horses find it. They'll sense where it is and lead us to it."

"That's a good idea," I said.

I woke the others. We decided to turn loose my mare and free Abyad and Lightning.

Beauty went first. She sniffed the ground and then lifted her head and sniffed the air. She stood still for a while in the brightening light and then began to move, with the other two horses behind her. We followed, leading the other horses. Beauty had left the trail and was crossing a stretch of rocky land.

The sun had risen and began to beat down on our heads. It grew oppressively hot. There was no wind; the air hardly stirred. Beauty moved along, farther and farther from the trail. From time to time she lifted her head and sniffed the air.

"Look." Isma'in pointed. "She's found the bed of the *wadi.*"

Indeed, we were walking along the bed of the *wadi,* and green bushes were occasionally to be seen along its sides which sloped gradually upward, disappearing somewhere high in the hills.

"There is water up there," said Isma'in.

We walked on. The sun beat down from above and powerful heat waves rose from the earth. The horses plodded along. Another hour passed, and another. The mountains seemed to come closer. We could hear each other's heavy breathing, and the air whistled in the horses' nostrils. Suddenly Beauty broke into a light gallop. The other two horses followed her.

"There is water ahead!" Isma'in shouted. The rest of the horses began to whinny, and we hurried after Beauty.

"Wait!" Isma'in cried. "I see a camel train."

I stopped, took out my pistol, and ordered the others to ready their weapons. The camels' owners might be smugglers, and if they were, they would be heavily armed. We drew closer and could make out several Bedouin leading some ten camels. Isma'in went first, rifle in hand. We trailed him closely. Guns glistened in the hands of the Bedouin.

"*Saalem Aleikum,*" Isma'in cried.

"*Aleikum Saalem,*" the Bedouin replied: "Peace be with

you." We lowered our weapons. The Bedouin lowered theirs. This meant that they would not attack us.

"Is there water ahead?" Isma'in asked.

"In the water hole," they replied. "Right here."

We found two pools of sweet water in the shade of tall shrubs. Who knows who had dug them, and when? Desperate travelers and thirsty nomads, with their sheep, cattle and camels—these ancient water holes had surely, more than once, saved the lives of travelers such as we.

A rusty can attached to a rope was lying near one of the water holes. We lowered the can into the deep and it was a long time before we heard it hit the water. The tautening rope indicated that the can was filling. We pulled it up, full of clear, cool, fragrant water.

Water had never tasted so good. All my senses sprang back to life. After we had drunk our fill, we watered the horses. Then we gathered wood and lit a small campfire. We boiled a canful of water, and invited the Bedouin to have coffee with us. They gladly accepted. They brought

camel yoghurt and *pitot*—desert bread, dry and tough as leather. We ate the *pitot,* sipped the coffee, and felt our strength returning.

The Bedouin told us that the oasis of Ein Portaga, on the road to St. Catherine's, was only a day's journey away. They wished us well, and their caravan continued northward. Following the traditions of the desert, we did not ask what they were carrying in the sacks that lay on the backs of their camels.

As they disappeared into the distance, we began to wash ourselves. The cool water refreshed our weary bodies. The horses ate the shrubs and whinnied with pleasure. We laughed and joked again.

We decided to travel as far as Ein Portaga that night and to rest there for a day. Isma'in would lead us. He knew the way.

Ein Portaga is a beautiful oasis in the heart of the desert. It has a bountiful spring, whose waters nourish tall trees and lush grass. An old Bedouin lives there. He grows vegetables, which he sells, earning his livelihood "with the help of Allah, the great and the merciful."

We spent the day in the shade of the palm trees, enjoying a welcome respite after ten days of hard riding. The horses grazed and gathered strength for the rest of the journey. Refreshed, we continued on our way to the monastery of St. Catherine.

8

A Raid

We had stopped for the night still two days' ride from
St. Catherine's. The heat wave was over and the nights
were cold and clear. I was wrapped in my blankets, fast
asleep. We had camped at some distance from the water
holes, which were at the foot of granite hills, to avoid
being surprised by bandits who might stop to water their
animals.

Suddenly I felt someone shaking me. I woke up and
reached under my saddle, which I was using as a pillow,
for my pistol.

"Get up, Abu-Gil." I heard a voice whisper.

"Who is it?"

"Isma'in. Something's happened."

I knew that Isma'in wouldn't wake me without good
reason. I got up and put on my boots.

"What is it?" I asked.

"I was out hunting near the water holes. Gazelles usually come down from the hills for water toward morning. I was lying hidden, hoping to shoot one. Suddenly—only a few minutes ago—I heard hoofbeats. My ear was close to the ground, so that I heard them from afar off. There must be about thirty horsemen. I'm afraid it's a troop of Bedouin looking for booty."

There are bands of Bedouin led by their sheikhs or their eldest sons who swoop down on passing caravans and carry off whatever they can lay their hands on. The hard-pressed nomads try to live off their flocks, but what sheep and camel don't provide, they take by force of arms.

"We must find out what they're up to," I said.

We removed our boots and wrapped our *kefiyas* around our feet to muffle the sound of our footsteps. Then we put on our burnooses, the desert robes which are the color of granite at night. We blackened our faces with ashes from the campfire so that they wouldn't stand out in the dark. Then we loaded our pistols.

"Let's go," I whispered to Isma'in.

My Druze friend walked a step ahead of me. He moved on cat's feet, pressed against the rocky hillside so that he would not be silhouetted against the night sky. I followed suit, and we made our way down the narrow path that led to the water hole, careful not to dislodge stones that might give us away.

Suddenly Isma'in whispered into my ear: "There are the horses!"

We fell to the ground. Ahead we could see several horses with armed riders on their backs. Their rifles glistened. There was silence, except for the wailing of a desert fox.

The riders were speaking Arabic.

72

"They are camped up there, Sheikh Ja'afar," we heard one of them say.

"Right," said the man addressed as Sheikh Ja'afar. "We'll wait here and attack them at dawn. If we strike suddenly, we can take everything they have."

"Yes, my Sheikh," said the first speaker. "But we don't know how many they are. All we've seen is their campfire."

"Right, Muhamad Abu-Uda. But we are many, and well-armed. With the help of Allah, we will succeed."

"*Inshallah*—God willing," said Abu-Uda.

The horsemen dismounted, and we saw them stretching out on the ground to wait for dawn. I put my hand on Isma'in's shoulder to indicate that it was time to return to our camp. The bandits rested silently, their black burnooses invisible against the dark ground.

We stole our way back. Luckily, the wind was blowing in our direction, so the Bedouins' horses hadn't scented us. Otherwise they would have let their masters know we were there.

We got back to camp and woke our comrades. It would be light in half an hour. We had to move before dawn.

We worked quickly and silently. We rolled up our blankets and saddled the horses with special care. A loose saddle girth can cost you your life when you're on the move. Then the mule was loaded and tied to Isma'in's horse. In a matter of minutes we were ready to set out. We piled wood on the fire to keep it burning so that the Bedouin would think we were still there. At first we moved slowly, hoping our hoofbeats would not be heard.

It began to grow light. First the hills could be seen;

then we were able to make out individual objects. A fox scrambled over the rocks.

We descended the hillside and began to cross a broad valley. I rode at the head of the party and Isma'in, leading the mule, brought up the rear. I spurred my horse and we all broke into a slow gallop. I was still urging Beauty on when Isma'in drew up alongside me and shouted, "They are after us!"

I looked back and saw a cloud of dust kicked up by the band of horsemen just coming over the top of the hill.

"Follow me!" I shouted and dug my spurs into Beauty's ribs. She broke into a racing gallop, and the rest of the horses followed. A cloud of dust rose from under their hooves. Stones and gravel flew upward into our faces. The dust enveloped us. At least our pursuers wouldn't be able to tell how many of us there were.

The horses galloped forward across the valley. Bullets whistled in the air around us. But we were moving too fast for them to hit us.

I looked back and saw that they were gaining on us. Our horses were worn out by the long journey southward and would not be able to sustain their pace for long. We would have to find a convenient hilltop and dig in for a fight. We had scattered across the valley in a long, unconnected chain. Isma'in, leading the heavily burdened mule, had fallen behind. The mule was a fine beast, but she couldn't move as fast as our thoroughbreds. Fortunately we were nearing a hill at the far side of the valley.

"Up that hill!" I cried, spurring Beauty on. We had only a little way to go. Beauty galloped up the hillside and I dismounted. After me came Dana, Gil on Lightning, and the rest. Isma'in and the mule were last.

We prepared for battle. We hid the horses behind an

outcropping of rocks and put Gil in charge of them. He held their reins and was to soothe them when the shooting began so that they would not panic. The men took their places behind rocks and shrubs. They were to hold their fire until I signalled them to shoot. It was better to deliver one deadly volley than to waste ammunition by firing at random. We might have to wage a long battle, and every bullet would have to count. We sighted the riders below, cocked our guns, and waited. When the time came, gunfire would rain down on the enemy.

The hill, which had echoed with hoofbeats, was suddenly still. It seemed deserted. There was no sign of the handful of men who waited with throbbing pulses for whatever might come.

I looked out from behind a big rock, prepared to give the signal. The horsemen were galloping toward us, in a loose line, their *kefiyehs* fluttering in the wind, brandishing curved swords and long-barreled rifles. We could hear them calling to each other, urging each other on.

Sheikh Ja'afar rode at their head on a handsome gray mare. The sheikh had a fine black beard and was dressed in a splendid burnoose. As they came closer, we saw flushed faces, swords swung high, rifles ready for action. In a moment they would reach the hilltop. I raised my arm and cried:

"One volley—fire!"

Seven rifles thundered as one and were silent. Fire spurted, bullets thundered, smoke rose—and all was still, as before.

Bewildered, their horses pulled up short, turned tail, and fled. Two bodies—wounded or dead, we could not tell —were left behind on the ground, and two men were running downhill on foot, their horses having fallen under them. A riderless horse galloped away, its saddle askew.

We had won the first round. We had gained time—only time. We were in bad trouble. They outnumbered us six to one. I estimated there were about forty of them. If they were smart, they could outflank us, and set siege to the hill. We had no water and no food. We couldn't hold out for long.

The riders pulled up beyond the range of our fire. We saw them huddled around their leader, talking. One of them, a bold one, rode towards us, waving his clenched fist and cursing us roundly. He seemed to be a relative of one of the casualties. The law of blood vengeance demanded blood for blood. He was letting us know that even though we had not started the fight, he would avenge his relative's blood in the end.

I saw Isma'in grab the butt of his military rifle, squint an eye, and aim at the rider through his gunsight. The rifle "froze" for a second; it seemed almost part of Isma'in's body. Then the powder flamed and thundered, and a bullet whistled through the air. The horse reared, threw its rider, fell to the ground, and writhed in death agonies. The rider, having fallen, sprang to his feet, and ran toward his band.

I sat, wondering what to do next. Suddenly I heard Jezreeli's voice: "Yirmi! I have an idea."

"Let's hear it. I'm at my wits' end about what to do."

Jezreeli crawled over to me. "Listen," he said. "These riders have no idea how many of us there are. If we can get them to think we're a big party, they'll leave us alone. All they want is booty; they're not interested in losing more of their men."

"Right. This is a raid, not a war."

"This is what we can do," he went on. "We have an axe. Let's cut big branches off the shrubs on the hillside. We can tie them together and make two huge brooms out of them. If we tie each of them to a horse and one rider gallops down each side of the hill, they will raise a huge cloud of dust. The bandits will think columns of riders are closing in on them from both sides. Then we can ride down the center, five of us abreast, shooting and shouting. I'm sure they'll panic and run."

"That's a good idea," I said.

"There's no time to lose," Jezreeli urged. "We've got to act quickly."

I called Hasson, Zevulun, and Srulik. With their knives and the axe, they cut the biggest boughs they could find. Isma'in and I kept watch. I told Gil to tie the horses to one of the rocks so that he could help cut branches.

By the time we had tied the branches together and made two big "brooms," the bandits seemed ready for another attack. This time the element of surprise was on their side.

Hasson and Jezreeli brought their horses. We tied the brooms to their saddles with long ropes, so that they could sweep as much ground as possible. Hasson rode to the right, Jezreeli to the left. They loaded their rifles and placed them in front, on their saddles. We led the rest of the horses to the other side of the hill and mounted them there, so that the Bedouin couldn't tell how few of us there were. I pulled out my pistol and shot a couple of bullets into the air.

Hasson and Jezreeli spurred their horses and rushed madly down the hill. The brooms dragged over the ground, raising great clouds of dust, so that Hasson and Jezreeli couldn't be seen. It actually looked as though two columns of riders were charging downhill, one on each side of the Bedouin band. From time to time the enemy could glimpse a horse's head, a flying tail, a black burnoose or a white *kefiyeh*. It looked like a full-fledged cavalry attack.

Then the rest of us rode downhill, five abreast. I rode in the center, with Gil alongside me. He looked serious and intent. This was his first experience in a shooting raid.

The two clouds of dust advanced toward the bandits. They mounted their horses, waiting to meet us with fire. Hasson and Jezreeli fired their pistols rapidly. The rest of us galloped over the hilltop together and raced the horses downhill. We shot into the air, rapidly and at random, trying to make as much noise as we could. The effect was stunning. A blood-curdling medley of shots and shouts rose from our midst. The mass of galloping horsemen seemed about to ride down the band of horsemen ahead. All this, augmented by the "columns" converging on its flanks, had the expected effect.

The bandits turned tail and fled.

I stopped and gathered my men around me. Hasson and Jezreeli rode up. Our faces were flushed. Gil's eyes sparkled with excitement.

We watched the cloud of dust kicked up by the fugitive bandits.

"Cowards!" Hasson said, contemptuously. "They're chicken. Worse than a coopful of hens."

We turned and rode back up the hill, where the mule was still tied to a rock. Then we continued on our way toward the monastery. In only two days we would reach St. Catherine's, and—hopefully—we could find the key to the mystery of the Pasha's treasure.

9

St. Catherine's Monastery

It was late afternoon when the monastery came into view, looming magnificently on the plain of Paran. The monastery lies at the edge of a stretch of this fertile plain which begins near the right fork of the Red Sea and stretches for about fifty miles into the heart of the desert. It contains tall palm trees, vegetable gardens, and fruit trees, and is watered by numerous springs.

The monastery itself is square, surrounded by a high wall to protect it against attack. Jebel Katerina—Mount Catherine—rises behind it. Very poor Bedouin who work the monastery lands live nearby.

There are two gates in the southern wall of the monastery. In periods of danger, these gates are shut and heavily bolted; at such times, you enter and leave the monastery by means of a unique "elevator." On the western side of the edifice, connected at a right angle to the wall, about forty-five feet off the ground, is a small hut-like construc-

tion. It contains a wooden cage that is hung from a heavy rope attached to a pulley.

The pulley is worked manually, by means of four handles on its face. Four monks turn it counter-clock-wise, winding the rope around the pulley, to lift the cage off the ground. When the pulley is turned clock-wise, the "elevator" descends.

The building was bathed in the last rays of the setting sun as we approached. It looked like a legendary castle; at any moment one expected to hear the blast of a hunter's horn and to see a great throng of huntsmen burst from its gates. But shadows creeping down from the mountain slowly engulfed the scene and the enchanted vision disappeared.

A short time before we reached the monastery, I halted our company, opened one of the sacks on the mule, and took out a British army uniform, carefully pressed and protected from creasing by a pair of boards.

I found a secluded spot, shed my burnoose and my riding boots, and donned the uniform. I put on a military hat and a pair of glistening military boots. When I returned, I was the very model of a British Army Colonel. I had pasted a carefully made beard on my chin and held an officer's baton in my right hand. There was a revolver in a shining leather holster at my hip. This costume had been prepared for me by Ruby and Yohai.

"I am happy to present the newest member of our party," I said. My friends, who were resting on the ground, stared at me in astonishment. "Colonel Smith," I said, and bowed politely. "Officer in His Majesty's Colonial Forces, member of the Royal Academy of Science, Historical and Archaeological Division, etc., etc., etc."

They gaped at me, and then burst out laughing. Zevulun, hardly able to speak, finally howled.

"His Majesty's officer! Ha, ha, ha! Have you ever seen the likes of it? I wouldn't have recognized him in a million years! I almost jumped to attention at the sight of him. Ha, ha, ha!"

"You look so strange, Father," Gil said.

Even Dana looked at me peculiarly. I smelled like her master, but I certainly did not look like him!

I told them all to address me as Colonel Smith as long

as we were in the monastery. I spoke English well and could easily pass—with the monks at least—as a British officer who had come to see their library. As an orientalist, it would seem natural that I spoke Arabic. The rest of the company were to play my helpers, my guards, and my servants. I warned Gil to be careful not to call me "Father."

When we arrived at the monastery, I headed the party on my mare, surrounded by my men. We rode up to the gate. The times were peaceful, and the gates were in use.

I called out to announce our arrival. A lean old monk in a frayed gray cassock, with tattered sandals on his feet and a round black hat on his head, appeared and asked what I wanted.

"I am Colonel Smith of His Majesty's Colonial Forces," I said. The monk had no idea what I was saying. Most of the monks spoke Greek or Arabic. But I wanted to impress him and so I spoke English.

I turned to Srulik, whom I had decided to make my lieutenant, and said something to him in English. He turned to the monk and said in Arabic: "His Excellency, Colonel Smith, Fellow of the Royal Academy of Science, and himself a distinguished scientist, wishes to see the Father Superior on an urgent matter."

"At once, at once," the monk replied. "I will open the gate immediately."

He took a huge key from the key ring at his waist and opened the massive, creaking gates. We entered the monastery courtyard, and the monk locked the gates behind us.

The courtyard was surrounded on all four sides by blocks of cells where the monks lived, as well as guest rooms, and galleries filled with works of priceless art. The courtyard itself was paved with stone slabs and contained several chapels and storage buildings. On the western side stood the "house of death," which was in fact a unique kind of cemetery, containing the bones of all the monks who had died in the monastery. It was the custom to bury the monks immediately after they died and to dig up the bodies after a year. The skulls were placed in one pile, and the rest of the bones were carefully laid out along the walls. An ancient monk sat in the entrance of the "house of death." He was distinguished for his venerable piety but looked like the Angel of Death himself.

On the north side grew a tall bush, bearing yellow flowers, which the monks believed to be the burning bush of the Bible, Moses' bush that burned and burned and was not consumed. It was also believed that Jebel Mussah was Moses' Mountain, or Mount Sinai, where the Jews had received the Law on their way from Egypt to the Promised Land.

Jebel Mussah was the site of a church named for Miriam, Moses' sister, as well as another named for Elijah the Prophet; and a third, at the very mountain top, the name of which I have never been able to learn. In the vicinity is also the spot where it is believed the Golden Calf was buried.

We were still standing there admiring the ancient monastery with its high bell tower when the monk with the keys came hurrying back, followed by a tall, dignified priest with a white beard, a high, pointed black hat, and a heavy cross around his neck. He walked with his hands clasped in front of him, in a posture of austere piety.

"Father Gregory, Bishop of the Orthodox Church," he

said to me in English. "Father Superior of the monastery."

"I am honored to meet you," I said, and bowed ceremoniously. "Colonel George Smith, officer in his Majesty's Armies, member of the Peerage, and Knight of Malta, historian, archaeologist, and member of the Royal Academy of Sciences, now serving in His Majesty's Forces in the Middle East," I introduced myself and handed him a number of documents from the flat leather portfolio I was carrying. They had been prepared for me by Yohai's men in Haganah Intelligence.

Father Gregory looked at my credentials and said, "It is an honor to receive you here. Follow me. We will show you to your quarters."

He turned and we followed him. Bedouin servants took our horses to the stables.

Strangers are well received at St. Catherine's, which extends its hospitality to all who ask it. My friends were given rooms with comfortable deep-mattressed beds and warm blankets. The nights are very cold in this region. Sometimes even in the mornings the ground is covered with silvery frost. It melts within a few hours and the earth grows hot underfoot. I was given a handsome room with a table, chairs, a fine bed, and a green-shaded kerosene lamp.

I didn't tell Father Gregory that evening why I had come. I was his guest, and it would have been unseemly to intrude my business so soon.

We rested in our rooms for a while. It was delightful to sink into a soft mattress after so many nights with nothing but a blanket between our weary bones and the stony desert ground.

Later that evening, Father Gregory invited me to his room. It was simply furnished with a narrow iron bed, a table heaped high with books, a big cross on the wall, and three unupholstered chairs. I sat in one of them, facing Father Gregory, and smoked my pipe. Dana, who had refused to leave me, lay at my feet. She placed her head on her forepaws and occasionally her stomach rumbled. Father Gregory told me the history of the monastery.

The monastery of St. Catherine had been built by the Byzantine Emperor Justinian in about 520 A.D. in an area sacred to both the local Bedouin and to Christians.

The summit of Mount Catherine, not far from which the monastery is located, is 8,800 feet above sea level. The monastery itself stands on about two acres of ground and is 5,093 feet above sea level. It was conceived as a fortress from which its inhabitants could defend themselves against attack by desert marauders.

The monks live according to very ancient regulations, set down by St. Vassily in the fourth century. The monastery buildings include a large church; the tomb of St. Catherine; saints' chapels; and a library containing valuable old manuscripts. The manuscript of an old version of the Septuagint, known as the Sinai Version, has been preserved in the library for centuries. There are Greek and Syriac manuscripts and old travel books.

A medieval mosque stands near the monastery gate, bearing witness to the friendly relations between the Christian monks and their Moslem neighbors through the ages. A cross within a crescent, the symbol of Islam, conspicuously adorns the outer wall of the mosque.

Smoking my pipe in silence, I sat and listened to Father Gregory. When he had finished, he showed me the monastery guest book, which contained the signatures of the many famous people who had visited there. One was the signature of Napoleon Bonaparte, who had stayed at the monastery during his Egyptian campaign.

It was already late when we bade each other good night. Once in my room, I lay in my broad, soft bed and thought about how I would go about locating the map we had come so far to find.

10

The Ancient Prayer Book

I was awakened by the sound of bells. I went out onto a broad, vaulted porch and a marvelous scene met my eyes. The sun had risen, and its rays shone out from the top of a mountain to the east of the monastery, lighting up the mountain opposite it. At first the shoulder of the mountain was bathed in a wonderful pink light, which moved slowly downward, exposing boulders, caves, and shrubs till it finally reached the monastery's bell tower, whose bells quivered and tolled, calling the monks to morning prayer.

I was still standing on the porch, leaning on the rail, when a strange monk appeared. His arms were piously clasped in front of him, his face was lean, his eyes dark and furtive. He wore a hooded gray robe, girded by a ribbon with an iron cross at its end, and he was shod in ragged sandals that scuffled over the stones of the floor.

"Good morning, Your Excellency," he said to me in Arabic, his voice dripping honey and myrrh.

87

Most of the monks were Greek, but they had learned Arabic from their Bedouin neighbors.

"Good morning," I said.

"How is your Excellency feeling? Did you sleep well in our humble abode?" he asked unctuously.

"I slept well," I answered.

"My name is Father Christian," the monk said. "A humble servant in the ranks of our order."

"I am very pleased to meet you," I replied.

The little monk stood near me, smiling his sugary smile.

"It's a lovely morning, isn't it?" he asked.

"Yes, a lovely morning," I replied, wondering how I could get rid of the fellow.

"The monastery is a holy place, a very holy place," he said.

I didn't answer him, but fixed my eyes on the mountain opposite.

"People come here to pray, to worship the Lord," he said.

I didn't answer.

"And why have you come?" he asked. "Has your soul thirsted for the Lord, to worship Him, His crucified son, and holy St. Catherine?"

Again I refused to answer. "Excuse me," I said, "I must wash and dress for breakfast."

"Oh, yes, yes," he cried. "Hearty appetite, Your Excellency. Hearty appetite. Good morning, merciful Sir." He bowed, scraped, and vanished.

I shruggd my shoulders. I did not like this monk with his sugary smile. After breakfast, Father Gregory showed me around the monastery. He spent hours explaining the treasures its galleries contained. "These objects," he said, "are brought by pilgrims who come to us from the ends of the earth. They pledge them in times of trouble, when they hope that the sanctity of the monastery will intercede for them in Heaven."

We walked around the courtyard and stopped in front of the burning bush. Then the bishop showed me the "house of death," and from there he took me to the "elevator." On the way we met smiling Father Christian. He greeted the bishop and remained with us, exuding good cheer and helpfulness.

"What can we do for you, Father Christian?" the Father Superior inquired sharply.

"Oh, nothing, Holy Father. I saw our esteemed guest and came to hear what news he brings from the world."

"Go back to your cell, Father Christian," the bishop commanded. "Pray, and study the sacred books. Don't waste your time in idle conversation. A man's time is valuable. He shouldn't waste it in folly."

The monk's face flushed crimson with anger, but he immediately took hold of himself, saying, "As you command, Holy Father!"

When he had gone, the bishop turned to me and said, "That is his way. He assaults every visitor with questions. He came here about half a year ago, to do penance, he said, to atone for his sins. He asked to join the sacred brotherhood and spend the rest of his days praying, fasting, and engaging in sacred worship. I accepted him, but he doesn't seem to me a penitent at all. There is something peculiar about him that I don't understand. He is too slick, and he loves to eat, joke, and chat with every passerby. He asks endless silly questions. That's not how a penitent behaves."

I listened in silence and decided to beware of Father Christian. We returned to the bishop's room and sat talking. The bishop told me that a dangerous band of robbers had been operating in the area of late. They had looted the caravans of merchants and pilgrims and had mercilessly slaughtered some of their victims.

"And the odd thing," Father Gregory said, "is that they know exactly whom to attack. They leave poor people alone, and they don't bother the nearby farmers who depend on their labor—and our pilgrims' gifts—for their livelihood."

"And the police haven't been able to track them down?"

"No. Apparently someone warns them when the police are about to move in on them. They hide in the mountains, where they are hard to find. They've even ambushed a troop of mounted police and killed three of them."

"Father Gregory," I said, getting down to business at last, "in civilian life I am a lecturer at Cambridge on the history and archaeology of the Middle East. I am especially interested in manuscripts of old prayer books and missals. They teach us a great deal about history and the development of religion in various periods."

"Our library contains several manuscripts: the prayer books of St. Francis, of Bishop Leon of Crete, of Father Sebastian the Greek, of Saint John, Bishop of Rhodes, and others," Father Gregory replied.

My heart skipped a beat when he mentioned the prayer book of Father Sebastian. The map I was looking for would be in that missal—if the map existed at all.

We decided to look at the books together, to see which ones I might like to examine more closely. When we had finished talking and I opened the door to leave, I found

Father Christian standing outside. I could swear he had been eavesdropping.

"What are you doing here, Father Christian?" the bishop asked.

"I just happened to be passing, Father," he said, and left us.

I went to see how my comrades were getting along.

"A monk called Father Christian has been questioning us," Jezreeli said.

"He's been asking where we intend to go and when we're leaving," Srulik added. "And he wants to know what we're doing here."

"I told him to mind his own business," Zevulun said.

"We are guests here," I said. "We must avoid insulting Father Christian. He apparently finds life here dull, so he latches on to every visitor. Let him ask questions, all the questions he wants. They don't really do us any harm."

"We've reached the monastery, Yirmi," Jezreeli broke in. "And you still haven't told us why we've come."

"Right," Srulik agreed. "You said you'd tell us when we got here."

"Patience," I said. "I cannot tell you everything as yet. We must be careful. But I can say this: You'll soon know the whole story. Wait a few more days."

"All right," said Hasson. "We've waited this long; we certainly can be patient awhile longer. As they say, 'Patience pays off in the end.'"

That afternoon Father Gregory summoned me to the library. It contained many cabinets full of books and manuscripts. Gems and ornaments, set in brillant silver and gold, were displayed in glass cases. Precious ikons hung on the walls.

Father Gregory led me to a locked bookcase. He took out a key and opened it. It contained a row of ancient manuscripts. He removed several of them and laid them on the table.

"These," he said, "are manuscripts of old missals."

He read the names of their authors. I chose three, among them, of course, the prayer book of Father Sebastian. I placed them on the table, and Father Gregory put the others back into the cabinet.

"I'll sit here and study them," I told him.

He locked the cabinet door and left me alone.

Father Sebastian's prayer book was very large; its parchment pages were yellow with age, tattered and stained, and covered with old Latin script, which I could barely decipher.

The volume was bound in heavy parchment. If the map were hidden in its covers, I would have to pick them apart to find it. I had brought with me a sharp little knife and a bottle of glue.

I was still examining the book when I sensed someone behind me. I turned and saw Father Christian.

"What are you doing here, Father Christian?" I asked him.

"I've come to study the wisdom of the ancients," he said.

"Then why are you standing behind me?"

"By chance, merciful master. I just happened to be here. I want to read one of these books."

He took a heavy volume from a shelf and sat down to read it. I waited for him to finish and leave. It would be foolish to succumb to my impatience at this point. We had come a long and dangerous way to find Father

Sebastian's prayer book. Having found it, why ruin everything now?

I pretended to be reading the book. I wondered why our mysterious Sikorite had hidden the map in the monastery and how he had gotten back to Jerusalem afterward to record the story in that little black book. Why hadn't he taken the map back with him? Obviously something must have happened to make it necessary for him to leave it behind. Surely he had planned to return for it and for some reason had been prevented from doing so.

Father Christian leafed through the pages of his book. Finally he got up, put the book back on the shelf, and left. I looked around me. The library was empty. I slipped the knife and the bottle of glue out of my briefcase and studied the binding of the prayer book. I noticed that the right-hand cover had been split at the bottom and pasted together again. I slipped my blade into the crack and carefully pried away the glue. The layers of parchment separated, revealing a narrow opening with a sheet of paper that was folded deep inside. I was about to take it out, when I heard the sound of footsteps approaching. I quickly covered the missal with the second prayer book and pretended I was reading the third. It was Father Gregory, who had come to see how I was getting along. I told him how pleased I was with the books. He sat with me for a while and left.

My heart pounded with excitment. I looked around me to make sure that no one else had slipped into the great hall of the library. I slipped the knife into the opening in the binding and with it carefully withdrew the piece of paper. It was yellow with age and covered with peculiar diagrams. I put it in my briefcase. I then opened the bottle of glue and pasted the two layers of parchment together again. In a matter of seconds I was finished. No one would have guessed that the book cover had been tampered with. I put the knife and the glue back into the briefcase and continued leafing through the books. I was eager to get back to my room and study the map, certain that it was the mysterious clue we were looking for. But I couldn't hurry, lest I arouse suspicion.

At noon Father Gregory came to invite me to lunch in the refectory. I sat with the monks and we ate, and then I went to my room for a nap. Pulsing with excitment, I lay the map on the table and locked the door.

One side of the paper was covered with the same code I had seen in the little black book. Unfortunately Yohai had not supplied me with the key. On the other side was a map.

I studied it carefully. At the top were arrows indicating the points of the compass. Noted at the bottom, on the right, was St. Catherine's with Jebel Katerina next to it. Mount Moses was easy to identify. A winding road led northward from the monastery through the mountains until it reached a peak enclosed in a circle. This, it seemed to me, was Mt. Sarabit, north of Mt. Moses. Three arrows radiated from a black spot on the mountain side.

One of them pointed south, to a small church at the top of a mountain. A second arrow pointed east, to a drawing of a tree. The third pointed northeast toward one of a jutting crag. Something in code was written alongside each of these landmarks and inside the circle as well.

I studied the map all afternoon and came to the conclusion that the treasure must be concealed in a cave on the mountain which I assumed to be Mt. Sarabit, and that the cave was located within the area marked by the circle. The fact that a path seemed to lead directly there left little room for doubt. As for the three arrows, I assumed they indicated the exact location of the cave. Obviously a spot from which the church, the tree, and the rock would all be visible.

That evening I sat in Father Gregory's room. He was again talking about the monastery. I decided to ask about the people who had visited it over the years. I thought I might discover something about the person who had hidden the map in the binding of the old missal. I was convinced he must have been a Jew and had some connection with the Sikorites. I knew there was a big book in the archives, containing a chronicle of events that had taken place within the walls of the monastery. Perhaps it also contained the story of the unknown visitor who had hidden the map.

First we talked about pilgrims from across the Suez, who came to pray at the tomb of St. Catherine. Then Father Gregory told me about monks and nomads who had crossed the barren desert and had spent some time at the monsatery before moving on.

"Have Jews ever visited the monastery?" I asked.

"Very rarely. They usually prefer to camp outside its walls. But I have found three stories about Jewish visitors."

"That's it," I thought, but I betrayed none of my eagerness.

"Were they of any interest?" I said casually, puffing at my pipe.

"Only the last. The first of them came about a hundred years ago. He was a merchant whose caravan had been attacked by bandits and who had barely escaped with his life. His name was Sasson ben Shlomo Cohen. He was a cloth merchant from Baghdad, who transported his goods across the desert on camel-back.

"The second came from Yemen. His name was Sa'adiah Sharabi. He was looking for the Jews of al-Hibr, who lived like Bedouin, rode horses, tended flocks and were excellent marksmen. Traveling in the Arabian desert, he had wandered into the Sinai and reached us in a state of utter exhaustion. He stayed until he felt strong enough to move on."

Here Father Gregory stopped to rest. I puffed at my pipe and stroked Dana's head.

The old man breathed deeply and continued.

"The third Jew was the strangest of them all. According to the ledger he was wounded and bleeding when he came, his left hand having been shattered by a pistol shot. He was a young man and wore a beard and earlocks, like the very pious Jews. But he was also wearing riding boots and a burnoose, like a Bedouin, and was armed with pistol and dagger.

"He was found fainting outside the walls. He was brought in and given milk and water to drink. But when he revived and opened his eyes, he couldn't speak. He was apparently in such a state of shock that he had lost the power of speech. He lay motionless, his lips moving in silent prayer. The monks wanted him to remain in the monastery in the hope that they could convert him to Christianity. But they got nowhere. Sometimes he would sit in the library and read. He seemed to be a learned man."

"Did the monks discover his name, Father Gregory?" I asked.

"Yes. His name was Aharon ben-Avraham."

"And what happened to him in the end?"

"One day he disappeared, taking a powerful mule with him. He apparently intended to try to get home. Whether he succeeded or not, no one knows."

Father Gregory fell silent.

Could this mysterious young man, Aharon ben-Avraham, have drawn the map? It was all probably explained in the coded message that I could not decipher.

We spent two more days at the monastery. I went through a pile of old books in order to avoid arousing Father Gregory's suspicions.

11

The Kidnappers

At noon of the fourth day we thanked Father Gregory and rode out of the monastery gate. We were spared the presence of Father Christian, who for once was not around.

We decided to ride toward Mt. Sarabit, hoping to reach it by early evening and set up camp. When we got there, I intended to tell my companions about the Turkish Pasha and his gold, and to begin our search for it the following day.

We rode through a ravine leading northward. I carried the precious map in a leather pouch next to my skin. Our horses were fresh after their rest in the monastery and trotted swiftly over the sandy terrain.

We had traveled a long way before the sun began to set. It was blood-red and cast a deep glow over the sky. Great shadows sped over the desert. They seemed to stretch from our horses' hooves far out into the distant horizon. The trail twisted and turned around jutting boulders and conical hills. I remembered what Father

Gregory had said about outlaws in the vicinity and alerted my companions to the possibility of an ambush.

"I would like to lay my hands on those crooks," said Zevulun. "I'd treat them to a dose of hot lead. They'd remember me for the rest of their lives."

" 'Crime doesn't pay,' " Hasson said. "But everyone has to learn that for himself. They will, too, in the end."

"I'd just as well not run into them," Srulik said. "They're well armed, and any encounter will end in bloodshed. I hate bloodshed."

"Right," Jezreeli responded. "I don't like bloodshed either. But anyone who slaughters innocent travelers deserves what he gets. There's only one way to deal with such outlaws."

Srulik didn't reply. He rode silently on his stallion, sunk in thought. Srulik had always fought only when there was no other way out.

"We Druze have another way of looking at it," Isma'in volunteered. "We believe in killing anyone who tries to kill us. We prefer to live in peace, but when the need arises, we will fight to the death."

"That's what the Bible says."

"There's a proverb that says it too: 'If you want peace, prepare for war,' " Hasson added.

"Absolutely. It's a good saying," Isma'in agreed.

"I think differently," Srulik said. "If we always prepare for war, how will we ever find peace? How can you think about peace when war is always on your mind? If we lived according to your Roman proverb, Hasson, our swords would never rest in their scabbards, and the rifle would run our lives."

We went on riding in silence. Srulik's words, spoken so

solemnly, had set me thinking. Darkness began to engulf the desert. Only the pounding of hooves and the creaking of saddles could be heard. By the time we had reached the lower slopes of Mt. Sarabit it was night.

I chose a spot for our camp, and we dismounted. We were fresh and buoyant and enjoyed setting up our camp. One of us started unsaddling the horses, another spread blankets on the ground; a third got the food ready; a fourth unpacked the coffee pot; and one of us just crouched, gazing into the desert night.

I sent Gil to gather wood for the fire and warned him not to tarry. Then I took off Beauty's saddle, put it on the ground, and looked after Lightning. When both horses were unsaddled, I put some oats in their feedbags and hung them over their heads.

I took our blanket rolls and spread them on the ground. No Gil. I was annoyed with him. Why was he taking so long? We had to start a fire and cook something for supper. I was anxious now to tell my companions about the treasure, and that would take a long time.

I sat on a rock to rest and found myself thinking about what Srulik had said. "I know how he feels," I thought. "I too recoil from bloodshed. I prefer to live in peace. But I know that *someone* has to be prepared to take up arms when the need arises. If all of us were to shut ourselves up in our houses, like Srulik in his garden paradise, who would fight when fighters were needed?" I too wished the time would come when I could lay down my arms and rest. . . .

Suddenly I felt Dana tugging at my boots. She was restless and whimpering softly; from time to time she lifted her head and barked.

"Quiet, Dana!" I cried.

But she went on barking and looked in the direction Gil had taken. Her behavior surprised me.

"Quiet, Dana!" I ordered again. "What is all this barking about?"

But she would not stop and kept looking in the same direction. I began to be alarmed. Where was Gil? Why was Dana so restless?

I got up and paced back and forth impatiently. A man can usually keep a cool head whatever happens. But that's a little hard to do when your son is involved. Isma'in got up and came over to me.

"What's the matter, Abu-Gil?" he asked.

"I sent Gil for wood and he hasn't come back."

"Where did you send him?"

"That way, toward that clump of bushes over there."

"He'll probably be back in a minute," Isma'in replied. "Don't worry, Abu-Gil." And he went back to where he had been sitting.

But I couldn't calm down.

"Gil!" I called. "Gil! Where are you?"

Only an echo replied: G—i—lll!

Dana went on barking and fidgeted uneasily.

"I'm going to look for him," I said to Isma'in.

"Wait a minute. I'll come with you."

We took our revolvers and began to move toward the bushes. They loomed ahead, a dark threatening mass.

"Gil," I cried. "Gil! Where are you?"

There was no answer.

"Gil! Gil! Gil! Gil!"

"He's lost his way," I said.

"No," said Isma'in, hesitantly. "I don't think so."

"Do you suspect anything?" I asked, my heart almost standing still.

"Yes, Abu-Gil. I've been thinking about the thieves Father Gregory told you about."

"Impossible!" I cried. "You don't think they've kidnapped him?"

"It is possible," Isma'in said.

"How could I have been so stupid as to send him out by himself? My God! What an ass I am!"

"Keep calm, Abu-Gil." Isma'in said. "We're not even sure they have kidnapped him. In any case it will be impossible to find their tracks in the dark."

We returned to the camp. Everyone gathered around us. "Gil has disappeared," I told them.

"Could he have lost his way?" Zevulun asked.

"Possibly," I said.

"I think we ought to fire a couple of shots in the air. If he *is* lost, he'll hear them and head this way," Jezreeli suggested.

Jezreeli shot in the air three times. The shots echoed in the hills.

"Now, let's all yell 'Gil' three times, as loud as we can," Jezreeli said. He counted: "One, two, three" and we all shouted, "Gil! Gil! Gil!"

We waited, but heard only the echo of our cries reverberating in the darkness. Then the silence of the desert night closed in around us.

"I'm sure of it now," Isma'in said. "Spies from the gang must have followed us when we left the monastery. When they saw Gil leaving the camp, they must have ambushed him and taken him hostage—either for ransom money or to question him about our plans."

"This is what we'll do," I said after a long pause. "Isma'in can't follow their tracks in the dark, but Dana can. Everyone but Srulik will come with us. Srulik will stay behind and guard the camp. The rest of us will wrap our boots up in our *kefiyehs* to muffle our footsteps. We should be fully armed. Isma'in and I will lead the way. Zevulun, Jezreeli, and Hasson will follow at a distance. I'll take my two hand grenades; we might need them. There may be a great many men in their party, and our rifles may not be enough."

"All right."

I hugged Dana and whispered to her, "Dana—Gil is lost, Gil is lost." Dana whimpered miserably; she probably sensed my meaning, as animals do. "Help us find him, my lovely. Help us, won't you?" She whimpered again. "Now, show us the way. Quietly. Without a whimper."

I tied her to a leash and let her sniff Gil's *kefiyeh,* which he had left near the campfire. Then I whistled the signal she knew meant "Follow the track." Dana sniffed the *kefiyeh* again and seemed to understand what we wanted. She put her nose to the ground, sniffed around a bit, and began to tug at the leash.

I hitched the grenades to my belt, gripping my revolver in my right hand and the leash in my left. We walked softly. My old friend Isma'in was at my right. It was good to have him along at such a time. There is no one who can match him in a tight spot. He moves with a cat's stealth and his eyes are keen as an owl's at night.

Dana led me along a narrow, uphill path. The night was moonless and dark. Only the stars cast dim light over the silent mountains, the giant boulders, and the caves that gaped like the mouths of ugly monsters.

The path climbed upward. Dana moved along, pulling me after her as she sniffed the ground. We had walked for over an hour when Isma'in suddenly grabbed my arm. I bent over and got to my knees beside him. He examined the ground ahead and finally pointed to the right. The silhouette of a man stood out against the sky.

"A sentry!" Isma'in whispered into my ear. He crawled back quickly to warn the others. They froze in place, motionless. Isma'in returned and whispered, "I'm going to kill him."

He took off his boots. The soles of his feet were tough as shoe leather. Then he wrapped himself in my black burnoose and set his dagger between his teeth.

"Dont kill him," I whispered. "We want to take him alive."

Isma'in disappeared in the darkness ahead. I crouched against a boulder and thought how foolish the sentry was. Instead of hiding behind a rock or tree, he stood exposed against the sky—endangering not only himself but also his friends, who were depending on him. I wouldn't have liked to have a fool like him in my group, but thanked my lucky stars that he was one.

I sat in this way for several minutes, muzzling Dana with my hands lest she give us away. I watched the sentry's dark figure, knowing I could rely on Isma'in to deal with him.

Suddenly a shadow rose behind the dimly silhouetted guard. I saw a quick movement and heard a throttled gasp. Then all was silent. I got up and moved ahead, pulling Dana behind me. The rest followed. As we came up, Isma'in was tying up a big man who lay on the ground, his head bleeding. Isma'in had struck him a smart blow with the handle of his dagger. After he had tied the fellow's hands and feet with a rope, he tore a piece of cloth from his *kefiyeh* and gagged him. "Now he'll be quiet as a fish," he said.

We knelt alongside the man. He was a massive brute, but his brains obviously didn't match his brawn.

"I smell smoke," Hasson said, sniffing the air.

"They've probably lit a fire. They expect their sentry to warn them if anyone approaches," Jezreeli said.

We crossed the hilltop and began to descend into a little valley hidden among the crags. This was probably the only path into the valley, so they were willing to trust their sentry to warn them if anyone was coming. We came around a bend in the path and saw, not far ahead, a campfire with several men around it. I stopped.

"We'll surround them," I whispered, "and close in from all sides. I'll go first, with my pistol in my right hand and a grenade in my left. The moment you see me enter the circle of firelight, move in. Load your guns now and cock them. That will give us eight bullets for a starter. Make sure you don't hit Gil if we have to shoot," I added. "I hope we won't have to, but it's just as well to be ready. Each of us should cover two members of their party. If anyone moves, give it to him. I don't want them to hurt Gil."

I gave the others time to reach their positions. Then I began to move toward the fire. Dana was on her leash, and I muzzled her with my hand. She pricked up her ears at every sound.

I stopped and peered between two rocks. About ten men sat around the little campfire. Their weapons were strewn on the ground, and they were sitting at their ease. A tall man with a big moustache sat near the fire. He was apparently the leader; the others were silent when he spoke. They were drinking coffee that had been brewed in a smoke-stained pot.

Gil, his hands tied behind him, sat on a rock next to the man with the moustache. I could hardly stop myself from running forward to free him. He sat with his head down, and on the other side of him—I could hardly believe it and rubbed my eyes to make sure I was seeing straight —sat Father Christian, the monk from St. Catherine's!

"Scoundrel!" I thought. "So you're the spy!"

I freed Dana, knowing that she could take on one of the bandits if she had to. She was trained for that. More than once she had jumped a man who was reaching for his gun and had disarmed him, sinking her fangs into his hand.

I cocked my pistol. By then every one of my men was certainly in position. It was time to move forward. I got up and began to advance toward the fire, pointing my pistol at the leader of the band.

"Hands up!" I cried in Arabic. "You're surrounded. Anyone who moves will pay for it!"

I closed in from the west, Isma'in from the east, Hasson from the south, and Jezreeli from the north, his pistol clutched in his one hand.

The thieves sat fixed in their places, stunned. Where had we come from? How had we got there? They had been sure that no one could enter the valley without their knowing it. But Gil smiled happily and cried, "Father! I knew you'd come. They tried grilling me, but I haven't told them a thing!"

"Hey!" Zevulun cried. "Here's our old friend, Father Christian!"

"Yes. He belongs to the gang and lets them know when anyone leaves the monastery," Gil said.

It was an effort not to shoot the false monk on the spot. But I knew it was not for me to avenge his victims. We would have to turn our prisoners over to the desert police. The laws of the desert, to be sure, are different from those of ordinary society, but I have never killed a man in cold blood. And I never will.

We covered the robbers with our guns. Isma'in cut Gil's bonds. Gil got up and moved his hands.

"Oof!" he said. "My hands fell asleep. They tied them so tightly, they're numb."

I told Isma'in to heap the outlaws' arms in a pile and collect their daggers. Then Isma'in bound their hands behind them, tied them to each other, and sat them by the fire. Only Father Christian was tied separately.

"How are you, my slimy one?" Hasson asked. "After some fun, were you? You spindle-shanked, slipshod, crock-headed son-of-a-sea-cocking fool of a spy that you are!"

Father Christian's sugary smile had disappeared. He looked at me with startled, terrified eyes, and burst into tears. "Don't kill me, Colonel Smith. I'm a miserable man. They made me do it. They made do their dirty work for them. Don't kill me. I'm a miserable man."

"Shut up!" Zevulun shouted, his face flushing with rage. "Shut up, you slimy sea-slug!"

Father Christian writhed on the ground and continued to cry.

" 'When a hypocrite weeps, the seas overflow,' " Hasson observed.

The erstwhile monk looked so miserable that, against my will, I began to pity him. He was no longer a dangerous spy but a frightened, cowering man, convinced he was about to be killed.

107

I sat by the fire and suddenly felt very tired and hungry. I wanted to have some coffee and go to sleep. But I overcame my weariness. I told my men to bring the prisoners' horses. We gathered their arms, sat them on their horses, and returned to our camp, where Srulik was waiting for us.

The fire which should have been made so much earlier was not lit till midnight. We cooked ourselves a hearty supper, ate, and sipped our coffee. Then we spread our blankets for a good night's sleep.

"I'll tell you about our mission tomorrow," I said. "We're all very tired now, and we should get some sleep. I couldn't tell it to you now, even if you had the strength to listen."

We checked the prisoners' ties and arranged to take turns guarding them.

I rolled myself in my blankets and shut my eyes. It was cold. But even when I began to warm up, I couldn't fall asleep. I was too tense from the night's adventure. I opened my eyes and looked at Gil, who was sleeping beside me. He was safe and sound asleep. Dana was also sleeping, her head between her forelegs. I lay on my back and looked at the lofty, star-flecked sky. I remembered old times, old journeys, old friends who had fallen in battle, until at last I sank into darkness and slept.

12

The Church, the Tree, and the Rock

I woke up completely refreshed. Our captives were sitting by the remains of the fire. Hasson sat beside them, on guard.

I called everybody together to decide what to do with the prisoners. It seemed best to camp where we were for the day and send some of us back to the monastery with the prisoners so the monks could guard them until the police arrived. The prisoners sat, their hands tied behind them, their eyes fixed on us. They seemed to be afraid we would hold a kangaroo court and bring them to justice on the spot.

We helped them onto their horses and tied the horses to each other. I send Hasson, Isma'in, and Zevulun to escort them to the monastery. Srulik, Jezreeli, and Gil remained at the camp with me.

Our men returned toward evening. They told us how surprised Father Gregory had been at the sight of their strange party—the bound riders on horseback, guarded by armed men, who turned out to be his recent visitors. Father Gregory was happy the criminals had at last been caught and that friends and wayfarers could again travel safely to and from the monastery.

"He sends you his heartfelt thanks," Zevulun said.

"You should have seen him, beaming like the full moon," said Hasson.

As we settled ourselves around the campfire that evening, I said, "The time has come to tell you about the Turkish Pasha's treasure."

"Treasure? What treasure?" Zevulun asked.

"The treasures I know about are found only in books," Hasson added.

"Then you'll be pleased to learn," I said, "that you are now actually taking part in a treasure hunt."

"A treasure—like the one in *Treasure Island?*" Gil asked.

"Not exactly," I replied. "But no less valuable and no less important. Many years ago a brutal pasha held sway in Jerusalem. His name was Kemal Ata-Pasha . . ."

Their faces, flushed and eager, shone in the firelight as I repeated the story Ruby had told me. I told them about the shipment of gold and Yehoshua Halevi; about the society of the Sikorites and the young man, Aharon ben-Avraham, who had hidden the map in the library at St. Catherine's.

"And that's why we've come all this way?" Zevulun asked.

"Exactly."

"And where is the map?" Gil asked.

"Here it is," I said and took it out of the pouch.

The map was handed around. Everyone examined it.

"We'll start our search early tomorrow morning," I said.

We sat around the fire for a long time and talked about the treasure and the pasha who had amassed it and about what the next day might bring.

The sun had just risen when we got up. I had hardly shut my eyes all night. We were so near the goal of our journey, yet supposing the treasure did not exist?

The desert was golden in the early morning sun. Big, long-legged mice that looked like kangaroos fled into their holes when they saw us. Sometimes a fox slunk by. The sun was not yet beating down with its usual midday ferocity; it was pleasant to ride. Map in hand, I led our party along the path it indicated. We came around a turn and Mt. Sarabit was before us.

"That must be the church on the map," Isma'in remarked, and pointed to a church standing on a nearby peak.

"Now we must go on until we see the tree and the jutting boulder," I said.

The path began to wind its way up the southern flank of Jebel Sarabit. I watched for the solitary tree and the boulder. I caught sight of the tree when we reached the shoulder of the mountain, which was dotted with caves, rocks, and crannies. I kept the church and the tree in sight, and at the same time tried to locate the jutting boulder.

We rode along in silence. We were all tense. In a little while we would know if the map was accurate—if the treasure actually existed. We moved farther ahead and the boulder came into view, standing high and straight on a distant peak. It was so delicately poised that it looked as if it could topple into the abyss below at the touch of a hand. But the moment we had spotted the rock, the church disappeared from sight behind a nearby hill. We continued climbing and at last reached a spot from which all three landmarks were visible: the church, the tree, and the crag. Ten yards to the right or the left and we would lose sight of one of them.

"This must be the spot."

There were three dots on the map. We examined the mountainside. Three caves were visible. We decided to enter the first and explore it. If it were empty, we would try the second, and if there was nothing there, we would explore the third. If the third was empty ... But I was convinced we would find the treasure in one of the caves.

We dismounted and tethered the horses to nearby rocks. I took a big flashlight out of one of the sacks on the mule, as well as an iron pick and a shovel. Zevulun took the pick, I the flashlight, and Hasson the shovel. Srulik and Isma'in held their revolvers ready. Wolves and foxes sometimes live in caves like these and one has to be careful.

I explored the first cave with the beam of the flashlight. Bats fluttered frantically from wall to wall. The floor was covered with sheep droppings. The cave had apparently provided shelter for shepherds and their flocks on cold winter nights.

Now it was completely empty. Zevulun tapped the walls with the pick, checking for an invisible hiding place. The walls responded with a dull thud. There was nothing there.

"No treasure, no trove," said Hasson.

"Wait," I said. "There may be something in the second cave."

We poked the flashlight into the second cave. A pair

of green eyes glittered and a jackal came flying out of it.

This cave, too, was empty.

"I hope there's something in the third one," I muttered.

"So do I," Zevulun echoed.

"If we don't find the treasure ... " I said.

"As long as there's life there's hope," Hasson interrupted. "We're still alive, *hamdu-lillah*, and we'll find the treasure."

Everyone else was silent. Tension mounted. The treasure *had* to be in the third cave. We could not have come all this way to find nothing but bats and sheep droppings.

I turned the flashlight on again. This cave's entrance was smaller than the others'. We had to duck to get into it. First we crawled on all fours through a low, rocky passage. After a while the tunnel widened, but we still couldn't stand up.

"I'm sure the treasure is here," Gil whispered.

"Don't jump to conclusions," said Hasson, who was behind him. "Wait and see."

There was no sign of a treasure in the third cave either. It was as empty as the rest. We examined every corner, nook and cranny, and found nothing but pieces of stone, animal droppings, and repulsive, slimy moss.

"No treasure chests here," Hasson said. "No candle, no burning—no treasure, no pleasure."

"Strange," I said. "Is the whole story a lie? Or a fantasy?"

"Apparently," said Jezreeli.

"Maybe the gold was here once, and someone else got hold of it," said Srulik.

"That could be," said Jezreeli. "The caves are open. Anyone can enter them."

" 'Last one there is a bloody ass.' That's what the

proverb says," remarked Hasson. "We should have come fifty years ago."

We went out into the open air and sat on the ground in front of the caves. It was very depressing. We'd come all this way in vain. Someone had got there before us. That's the way it is. You search and search, and seek and seek—and find that someone got there before you. And by accident to boot. My friends, sitting on the ground beside me, were silent.

"Wait a minute," said Jezreeli suddenly. "Who said the treasure has to be in one of these caves?"

"Where else could it be? In the sky?" Zevulun asked.

"There's nothing here but these three caves," said Srulik.

"What do you mean?" I asked Jezreeli, a spark of hope kindling in me.

Jezreeli didn't answer immediately. He got up and walked toward the caves. We saw him studying the terrain. When he came back he said, "I know the place where the treasure must be."

"You know?" Hasson said. "Where? I don't see anything. No forests, no trees; no monkeys, no men; no cow, no calves; no..."

"Let Jezreeli speak!" I said. "You say you've found the spot? There's no other cave around. Where else can it be?"

"Who said there are no other caves?"

"We've seen none," Zevulun said. "Maybe you have X-ray vision and can see into the mountain..."

"No, but after you've worked in a machine shop for years," Jezreeli replied, "you get to notice small things other people don't see. Come with me and I'll show you something interesting."

We followed him along a very narrow path, circling the caves we had explored, and stopped near a great rock on the ground above them.

"The treasure must be here," said Jezreeli.

"Here?" Hasson asked. "Inside the rock perhaps? You'll say 'Open sesame!' and the mountainside will open and disclose a cave heaped full of sapphires and gold? Is that it, Jezreeli?"

"Not exactly, but sort of . . . " Jezreeli replied.

"Show us what you've found," Zevulun said impatiently.

"It's simple," said Jezreeli. "The rock doesn't belong here."

"Oh?" Hasson said. "It doesn't belong here! So where does it belong? Or can you move mountains by the power of your word? I don't understand why this *isn't* the place where the rock belongs."

"Up there," said Jezreeli, pointing to a spot higher up the mountain. "It used to be up there. To cover the mouth of that cave. If you look closely at the place where it used to stand, you'll see a little hollow which even the desert winds couldn't smooth away. Someone rolled it down from above. I assume Aharon ben-Avraham did it—probably before he got to the monastery."

"That makes sense," Zevulun said. "It may be that Aharon ben-Avraham didn't indicate the exact spot until he had hidden the treasure, to make sure that no one else would find it."

"Look here," Jezreeli said, pointing to the rock. "Someone put smaller stones under it to prevent it from rolling down the mountainside. Have you ever seen a boulder like this, with rocks under it?"

The boulder was indeed supported by stones and a

115

little mound of dirt. It leaned—massive, gray and heavy—against the side of the mountain.

"It may very well be," said Jezreeli, "that the Turkish Pasha and his men rolled the boulder over the mouth of the cave. Yirmi," he said, turning to me, "I don't think the Pasha could have smuggled the treasure to this place by himself. He would have needed help to get it here and put it in the cave.

"But I don't understand a lot of things," Jezreeli continued. "What was Aharon ben-Avraham doing here in the first place?"

"Meanwhile," said Zevulun, "let's move the rock."

"Three cheers for Jezreeli!" Hasson shouted. " 'Eagle's eyes and the mind of a fox.' Hurrah for Jezreeli!"

It wasn't hard to move the rock. Zevulun stuck his dagger under it and it moved a little, and when we had cleared the stones and dirt from under it, it rolled to the foot of the mountain, followed by a hail of stones and gravel.

We saw the mouth of a cave.

"This must be it!" Jezreeli cried. "This *is* it, Yirmi!"

I lit my flashlight and shone it into the mouth of the cave. The others followed me in. We stopped because of the low stone ceiling. At the end of a long corridor-like passage we came to a roundish "room." The flashlight flickered on its walls. It was hard to breathe; the place had been sealed up for so long there was almost no air. I felt a little dizzy and leaned against the wall till fresh air began to flow into the cave.

"There are the chests!" one of my companions cried.

We saw four big chests standing in a corner of the cave.

Part III

The End of the Journey

13

Northward

Cries of joy echoed through the cave at the sight of the treasure. With the flashlight in my hand I continued to explore the walls of the cave. Suddenly Zevulun cried, "Look! Those are human skeletons!"

And sure enough, skeletons in a variety of postures gleamed whitely against the walls. Hasson lifted a glittering object. "A Turkish rifle! I know such arms well!"

We counted seven skeletons in all. One of them was especially large; riding boots still covered the bones of its feet.

"That's probably the skeleton of Kemal Pasha," Jezreeli said. "He was very tall, according to the history teacher, wasn't he, Yirmi?"

"Right. He was a giant of a man."

We examined the rest of the skeletons. We found Turkish arms alongside three of them—apparently the Pasha's men. Near the others we found old-fashioned pistols and Greek rifles of a sort that the inhabitants of Palestine used to carry under Turkish rule.

"Who are these three?" Gil asked. "They're not Turks, are they, Father?"

"No, Gil," I replied. "I think these are the skeletons of three young Sikorites."

The remains bore witness to a terrible fight that had taken place decades before. It would seem that the three Sikorite youths and Aharon ben-Avraham had trailed the Pasha and his henchmen to this spot. They had probably surprised the Turks as they were hiding the treasure. Presumably, Kemal Pasha had not been able to transfer the treasure to a safe place abroad and had decided to hide it in the cave until he could find a suitable ship at A-Tur, a village on the coast, famous for its fishermen and its smugglers. They used their sailboats to run contraband goods to foreign ports. The Pasha may have intended to hire such a boat to transport his treasure to safety.

It seemed clear that shooting had broken out when the Sikorites surprised the Pasha and his men and that only Aharon ben-Avraham had survived. He had managed to get out of the cave, roll the boulder down to seal it off, sketch the map and get to the monastery. He had remained there until he recovered from his wounds and, for reasons not yet clear to us, had hidden the map in the monastery. Why hadn't he taken it with him when he left? We would learn the reason only when the writing on the back of the map was deciphered.

We had much work ahead of us. First we took the chests out of the cave. They were big, made of hard wood, bound with iron hoops, and firmly locked. When we had got them outside, Zevulun stuck the pickaxe under one of the locks and broke it open.

We were blinded by its contents. The sunlight was reflected by thousands of gold coins: Austrian crowns, English pounds, Russian rubles, French coins and Turkish coins, big coins and small coins, the exact value of which only a specialist could estimate.

"A fortune!" Zevulun cried, astonished by the sight of the gold.

"Think of the blood that it cost!" Srulik whispered. "Think of the men whose lives were lost pursuing it."

We stood around the chest for a while and feasted our eyes on its contents. Then we shut it. We didn't bother opening the others. We covered the lot of them with blankets and left two members of our party to guard them.

We took the skeletons of the three Jews out of the cave and buried them with stone markers on the mountainside. Srulik covered his head and said a short prayer. Gil gathered small stones and arranged them in a Star of David on each of the graves. We stood with our heads bowed, paying our last respects to the Turkish Pasha's final victims. Then we buried the others.

Afterwards, we considered what would be the best way to transport the treasure. We decided to buy six camels and to load them with sacks. Four would contain the treasure chests and the others food and water for the journey. We would then resell the camels in the northern Negev and turn the gold over to the Haganah.

I sent Isma'in and Hasson to buy the camels from Bedouin near the monastery. We had enough ready cash, but if the need arose, we could borrow from the treasure, which was worth enough to supply us with all the camels in the Sinai peninsula.

Isam'in and Hasson returned two days later. We

wrapped the chests in heavy cloth, put them in sacks, and loaded them on the camels.

At dawn the next morning our caravan started northward. Isma'in rode first, leading the camels. The rest of us followed, guarding our precious treasure. I sent scouting parties into the surrounding mountains and caves to make sure no ambushes awaited us.

Srulik even went into some of the Bedouin camps. He was so familiar with their customs that he was able to gather the necessary information without strain or danger.

We kept our caravan on a regular schedule. We would travel in the mornings and the evenings and rest during the heat of the day. Now that we had camels to carry our baggage, we were able to take along a tent in whose shade we could rest.

Caring for the camels, the horses, and the dog took a great deal of time. They had to be watered and fed; every now and then the camels had to be unloaded so that they too could rest comfortably.

We traveled rapidly, though a mishap almost overtook us—a great flash flood that came upon us in a *wadi*. It rains very rarely in the Sinai peninsula, but when it does, the water tends to collect in ravines and finally comes raging through a single *wadi*. In a matter of minutes the *wadi* is filled with an enormous quantity of rushing water that carries everything before it.

Fortunately we were alerted to the danger in good time. We saw heavy gray clouds and flashes of lightning to the west, where it was obviously raining. Then we heard the distant sound of rushing water. We hurried across the *wadi* and climbed up one of its steep sides in time to see a wall of water advancing at tremendous speed along its bed. Within a short time the entire *wadi* was flooded by swirling brown water alive with rocks, trees, and earth. Had we been in its path, our entire party would have been drowned.

We stood on the high bank and watched the terrifying yet splendid spectacle. Within a short time the waters subsided. Only a small stream trickled along the *wadi* bed, and that, too, soon disappeared. The *wadi* lay below us, clear and dry, looking as though it had never known water.

14

Daytime Visitors

Two weeks after we had returned from our journey, I sent letters to my friends, inviting them to a celebration in honor of the successful conclusion of our treasure hunt.

My companions came with their families. Everyone brought something for the feast and we had a royal banquet. We roasted a whole sheep over an open fire, drank coffee, and demolished a heap of watermelons.

We sat around campfires, told tales, raced our horses, and vied with each other on the shooting range. We celebrated as we had in the old days when we were Guardsmen. But now our families were with us, as well as two honored guests: Ruby and Yohai.

After we had eaten, Ruby got up to speak.

"I don't have much to say. I knew you would come through. When Yirmi Shattar starts something, you can depend on him to wind it up successfully."

"Don't exaggerate, Ruby," I said.

Our guests murmured their agreement, and Zevulun said, "Don't be so modest, Yirmi."

" 'Modesty becomes the wise.' But who said you're wise, eh?" Hasson added jokingly.

Ruby continued: "The Turkish Pasha's treasure has finally reached its rightful destination. I can assure you it will be put to good use. For obvious reasons, I cannot tell you just how, but you can depend on it that it will be used well.

"And now there is still one mystery I would like to clear up for you. I'm sure you've wondered why Aharon ben-Avraham left the map in the monastery, and why he never went back for the treasure. Our cryptographers have deciphered the coded message on the back of the map. Let me read what it says:

I, Aharon ben-Avraham, faithful son of Jerusalem, am writing these words, though I don't know whether human eyes will ever see them. I weep grim tears. My good friends Shlomo ben-Yosef, Zvi ben-Asher, and Moshe, son of Rabbi Naftali, met their death in the cave, fighting Kemal Pasha. I managed to hide the treasure in a cave and to roll a boulder over its mouth, lest some stranger chance upon it. I, Aharon ben-Avraham, am now in the monastery of St. Catherine. I am about to return to Jerusalem. I am hiding a map showing where the treasure is hidden in the ancient prayer book of Father Sebastian because I am not sure I will be able to get it safely back to Jerusalem. The desert is full of dangers. If I fall into enemy hands, the map will be lost, and my friends will not be able to find the treasure. With God's help I hope to reach Jerusalem. If I do, I will return with my friends to get the treasure and restore it to its rightful owners in Jerusalem. And you, kind stranger, if and when you read this message, know that I, Aharon ben-Avraham, fought

125

for the glory of God and the honor of His people. If you find the treasure, return it to its rightful owners. Do not touch it; it is not yours to take.

And may God aid me in reaching my city, Jerusalem.

I, Aharon ben-Avraham.

"And what became of Aharon in the end?" I asked.

"He seems to have got back to Jerusalem and to have managed to record the story of his adventure in the notebook that we found. But, as we know, the Sikorites never retrieved the treasure. It may be that after Aharon's companions were killed in the cave, they no longer had enough members left to entrust with such a mission. What became of Aharon himself? We don't know. I have combed through every document and record of the time and have found nothing. But he will go down in the history of our people as a valiant young man who was ready to die for his principles and his people.

"Nor have we been able to learn anything about what happened to the society of Sikorites. Did it go on operating after Aharon's return? We don't know. Perhaps someday we will find a record that will reveal the rest of the story. We have by no means given up the search."

Ruby finished and was silent. We, too, sat silent. For a moment it seemed to us that the figure of that courageous young man hovered somewhere in the darkness outside the circle of firelight. But slowly good cheer won out over the gloom that Ruby's last words had generated. We began to sing, softly at first, then louder, and the tray of coffee passed from hand to hand.

Glossary

Note: "h" is pronounced like the "ch" in "loch."

Abu-Gil Shatter (Ah-boo′ G(h)eel Shah-ter′), father of Gil, the brave; "Abu" means "father of"; Arabs are often addressed as the father of their sons.

Abu Uda (Ah-boo′ Oo′-dah)

Abyad (Ahb-yahd′), "Whitey"; a horse's name

Aharon ben Avraham (Ah-hah-rohn′ ben Ahv-rah-hahm′)

Ahmad Muhammad abu Talal (Ahh-mahd′ Moo-hah′-mahd ah-boo′ Tahl-lahl′)

al Hibr (ahl Hee′-ber), a tribe of desert Jews

Avraham Hai (Ahv-rah-hahm′ High)

Ayelet Hashahar (Eye-eh′-let Hah-shah′-har), a kibbutz in northern Palestine

Bab-al-Wad (Bahb-ahl-Wahd), place name, meaning "Gate of the Valley"

Boaz (Boh-ahz)

Dana (Dah′-nah)

Dinah (Deen′-ah)

Ein Harod (Ayn Hah-rohd)

Ein Portaga (Ayn Pour-tah′-gah), fountain of Portaga, an oasis

Gamila (Djah-mee′-lah)

Gil (G(h)eel)

Gilad (G(h)eel-ahd′)

Gittel (Ghittle)

Haganah (Hah-gah-nah′), "Defense"; an underground organization of fighters created to defend the Jewish community in Palestine. It later became the Israel Defense Army.

Halsa (Hahl′-tza), a village in northern Palestine

Hanegbi (Hah-nehg′-bee), Yirmi's name

Hanegev (Hah-neh′-gev), "The Negev": village where Yirmi lives

Hasson (Hah-sohn′)

Hatzbani (Hahtz-bah′-nee), a river in northern Palestine

Herut (Hay-root′)

Isma-in al Atrash (Ease-mah-een′ ahl Aht′rahsh)

Ja' a far (Djah'-ah-fahr)

Jebel Katerina (Je'-bel Kah-teh-ree'-nah), Mt. Catherine

Jezreeli (Jez-ray'-lee)

Jezreel (Jez'-reel)

Kedar Kay-dahr'), a place name signifying "east"

Kemal Ata-Pasha (Keh'-mahl Ah'-tah Pah'-shah)

Kinneret (Key-nehr'-ret), Sea of Galilee

Kollelim (Khohl-luh-lim'), organizations that dispensed charity to Jews in the old community of Palestine

Lod (Lohd), a place name, on way from Jaffa to Jerusalem

Mahanayim (Mah-hah-nigh'-im), a settlement in northern Palestine

Marar (Mah'-rahr), a Druze village

Mt. Mussah (Moose'-ah), Mt. Moses

Mt. Sarabit (Sahr-ah-beet')

Na'amah (Nah-ah-mah')

Paran (Pahr-rahn'), a plain in the southern Sinai

Reuven (Reh-oo-ven')

Rosh Pina (Rohsh Pee'-nah), a village in northern Palestine

Ruby (as in English)

Sa'ada (Sah'-ah-dah)

Sa'adiah Shar'abi (Sah-ah'-dyah Shahr'-ah-bee)

Sasson ben Shlomo Cohen (Sah-sohn' ben Shloh-moh' Coh-hayn')

Shomrim (Shom-rim'), name of an organization founded to protect early Jewish settlements from attack; also means "guards."

Shoshana (Shoh-shah'-nah)

Sikorites (Hebrew: See'-koh-ree-im'), a group of rebels against the Romans in Palestine at the time of Christ; a modern resistance group that took its name

Srulik (Sroo'-lick), diminutive of Yisrael

Suleiman Muhammad abu Salmah (Soo-lay'-mahn Moo-hah'-mahd ah-boo' Sahl'-mah), the Bedouin sheikh who gave Lightning to Gil

Talal (Tah-lahl')

Tarbin (Tahr-bean'), a Bedouin tribe

Yehoshua; Halevi (Yuh-hoe'-sho-ah Hah-lay'-vee)

Yirmi (Yihr'-mee), short for Jeremiah (Hebrew: Yirmiyahu)

Yisrael (Yis-rah-el')

Yocheved (Yoh-cheh'-ved)

Yohai (Yoh-high')

Yoram (Yoh-rahm')

Zevulun (Zuh-voo-loon')